FACING UNFAMILIAR GROUND

An EMP Survival Story

CONNOR MCCOY

Copyright © 2018 by Connor Mccoy

All rights reserved.

No part of this book may be reproduced in any form or by any electronic or mechanical means, including information storage and retrieval systems, without written permission from the author, except for the use of brief quotations in a book review.

CHAPTER ONE

EVER SINCE THE EMP EVENT, when night descended, the city had been dark and ominous. Even the full moon couldn't illuminate the streets in the depths of the city. Walking was a hazard that most people avoided. Only the bravest, the meanest, and sometimes the quick and cleverest dared venture out.

The three men on the street now were a combination, one who thought he was quick and clever in the clutches of two of the largest and meanest men in the city. Perhaps it was unfair to label them both as mean. While one enjoyed the power he wielded, for the other it was employment. A means to an end. As long as he was employed by the powerful, his family was safe. He did his job well, but he was not cruel.

They dragged the man caught between them farther into the shadows between two buildings, causing him to plead more frantically. He was desperate, struggling and twisting, trying to wrest his thin arms from the beefy hands of the larger men. But these men had dragged bigger, stronger, and tougher subjects down this street.

They turned into an alleyway, and the man's pleading dropped to a whimper as the walls closed in around them, along with the darkness. It was so dark now that the three could not see each other's faces. They turned again and started down a flight of stairs leading to the basement of an old concrete building. As they reached the bottom, torches on either side of the door illuminated a mural painted there.

A black and gray jackal's head had been painted there, the ugly yellow teeth closing in on the top of the door. Beyond the jackal were images of death that the men did not care to look at. Below the teeth was a sign that read *THE KOUPE TRIBINAL*. The quick and clever man stopped struggling and retched, his eyes rolling back in his head.

The door opened immediately at the tap of a knuckle and, once the three men were inside, closed behind them. They moved into a large empty room with a dais built into the far end. The walls around the platform were lit with candles, which left the people seated there in shadow.

The quivering man was brought before the faceless, nameless leaders of The Koupe Tribinal. He was dropped to the floor in front of the dais, where he landed on his knees.

CHAPTER TWO

Glen Carter sat watching the sunrise on the deck overlooking the pond next to his cabin and thought about leaving. He didn't particularly want to go, but he felt compelled, obligated by his profession, to rejoin the human race. The three young adults he'd begun to think of as his family had talked him into it. To be fair, Glen didn't think they meant to convince him to leave this place. They knew he thought of it as home. But the more they talked about how bad the cities had become, how there was a shortage of physicians of any kind, how people were suffering from lack of medical care, the more he felt he owed society a debt and now was the time to pay.

He sighed and got up, glancing around for any sign of his fox. Thank goodness he hadn't allowed her to become reliant on him. He didn't want her or her kits to suffer when he was gone. But he thought he'd ask Anthony to check in every so often. Maybe offer his cabin as a retreat from the stresses of town life. Anthony liked his alone time.

Glen slid open the glass door and entered the room that served as living and dining room. Christian, Mia, and Sally sat leaning over a map on the table, discussing the logistics of cross-country travel. It had been a while since the three of them had made their way from the city to Glen's cabin, and it hadn't been a direct route. They weren't sure of the details.

"I don't see any way around it," Glen said. "I can't in good conscious stay here while the people in the city are suffering. But that doesn't mean you three have to come. You can stay here at the cabin. Eric and Anthony would help you with anything you needed."

"And we can't in good conscious stay here out of harm's way when we talked you into it to begin with. If we'd kept our mouths shut, you wouldn't feel compelled to leave. So, we're going with you. Hopefully, we'll be able to keep you safe." Sally looked determined, and Glen knew better than to argue with her when her jaw was set like that.

"Can you be ready in two days?" he asked. "Or do you need longer?"

"I think we can manage," Christian said, "but why do you need so long?"

"I'm going down to the town to tell Eric I'm leaving, and to tell Anthony to keep an eye on this place." And to tell him the secret caches and gadgets that made the place invaluable in a world with little electricity, communications, or sanity. Although he didn't say that part out loud. It wasn't that he didn't want the trio to know the cabin's secrets, it was more that it would take too long to explain it all a second time. If they ever came back here, then Anthony could tell them.

He took off for the town a little after noon. He followed the path worn into the ground after he and the trio had helped Eric liberate the town from the tyrant who had taken over following the EMP solar flare. Families had been reunited, and many of the townsfolk had made the trek to the cabin to thank them. Anthony had been a frequent visitor. He wasn't that much older than the trio, and while Glen knew that he admired Mia's spunk, it was Sally who he spent the most time with.

This trip was going to put an end to that budding romance. It was too bad Sally wouldn't stay behind. But Sally wouldn't leave Mia, and Mia wouldn't leave Christian, so for the time being, they were a unit. The trio who never would break out into duos, or reach for a solo.

Glen grimaced. That ripple effect was well overworked.

The town looked much as it had under Tyrell the Terror's rule, except the guards who met him at the gate were welcoming. He chatted with them briefly and then made his way to the Town Hall, where Eric had his office.

Glen almost was surprised to find him there. Quite often, when Glen arrived, he would discover an assistant sitting at the desk in the waiting room, whose primary purpose was to tell people looking for Eric where he might be found. Today, the desk was empty, and the door to Eric's office was open.

"Eric," Glen said as he walked in. "You aren't out inspecting your town today?"

Eric stood and offered his hand for Glen to shake. "No, I'm giving my people a break," he said. "Everyone needs a day to slack off every once in a while. Even me." Eric smiled as he sat back down in his chair. "What brings you down to New Town? Problems on the mountain?"

"No, no problems. At least not physical ones. I'm having a crisis of conscience. The kids have been telling me about post-EMP life in the cities. There is a shortage of physicians that I'm feeling compelled to help fill. I'm leaving the mountain, and it may be some time before I come back, if I come back at all."

"You'll be leaving us without a surgeon," Eric said, "doesn't that wear on your conscience some?"

"But you have a doctor. Everyone here has access to medicine and your doctor. He even stopped drinking when Tyrell died. I almost said when Tyrell left. There's a euphemism for you." Glen laughed uneasily. "My point is, you'll be okay. The town is well taken care of. Many people in the cities are not. I'm going to see if I can help. If I can't, I'll return."

"If you are able to return," Eric said, frowning. "My advice would be to stay here and save yourself. You are doing the world a favor by being independent. Who knows what will happen out there? The stories I've heard aren't pretty. They've kept me in small town America and, as you know, that wasn't a picnic either."

"I can't. I wish I could stay. But I have this highly specialized training, which I don't have to charge for anymore, money being worthless. I owe a debt to society. I took an oath." He sighed. "And frankly, if I could be talked out of this, the trio would have done it. They were quite persuasive."

"The trio? Is that what you are calling that motley crew you've grown attached to? Why don't you just call them 'my kids'? It's true enough." Eric walked out from behind his desk. "Come on, I'll walk you out. I've been sitting on my ass all day."

They walked through the marble building, with its beautiful wooden balustrades and polished floor. It echoed with emptiness, most of the departments that used to be housed here not pertinent to post-EMP living.

"Where can I find Anthony?" Glen asked as they stepped out into the crisp spring air. "I'm going to offer him the use of the cabin while I'm gone."

"Do you really think you'll be coming back?" Eric asked. "It's tough to get out of here, harder to get back, I'm told."

"Don't know," Glen said, "but I don't like to think of it as permanent. Psychologically, it makes leaving easier if I'm planning on coming back."

Eric nodded sadly. "Anthony is out at the north wall," he said. "He's supervising repairs."

The men said their goodbyes and shook hands again before Glen set out for the north wall. His path took him down Main Street, past the pharmacy he'd robbed and the street that ran to the library, where he'd met Terror and been knocked unconscious during the last fight over ownership of the town. He had conflicting memories of the town now. There were good memories overlaying the bad.

He'd helped inventory the pharmacy and set up protocols for the use of limited medicines once the fight was over. He'd spent hours in the library reading both fiction and non-fiction before they'd returned up the mountain to the cabin. And, on many occasions, he'd been invited to dinner in the house where he'd been confined to a closet. Those didn't obliterate the other memories but, laid overtop them, left him with a bittersweet feeling toward the town.

He found Anthony puzzling over a structural flaw in the corrugated metal wall that was the town's northern perimeter. Someone or something had split the metal in what looked like an effort to leave the community.

"Hell," Anthony said, "usually it's something or someone trying to get in. This looks like something that was in really wanted out."

Glen agreed. "Isn't it the norm? Can I take a few minutes of your time?"

Anthony spent a good half hour listening to Glen without interruption. When Glen was done, Anthony whistled a sign of his admiration for how Glen had adapted the cabin for a hostile environment.

"So, you'll watch it for me? Use it until I come home? Keep an eye out for the fox?" He didn't tell Anthony that he'd named the fox and her offspring, that seemed a little too crazy cat lady to admit to.

"Of course," Anthony agreed. "I will be grateful for a place to go. I'm at home in this town, but there is no room for solitude here. And it's a little too much like domestication. The cabin will make a welcome reprieve. But do come back, Glen. Don't lose yourself in the city."

On the way back to the cabin, Glen wondered if Anthony meant don't get yourself killed in the city, or don't forget who you are. Maybe both. Anthony, for all his outward appearances, was a thoughtful man. Deep. But it was hard to see past the army pants and boots and his heavily muscled and tattoo-covered upper body. He had himself well disguised. Anthony was a Renaissance man. Just when you thought you had a handle on who he was, he'd surprise you with a skill unrelated to anything you'd seen him do before.

"We've mapped out a route to the shuttle pick-up point," Mia said when Glen returned. "But it's a two-day walk, and we don't know what days they stop there."

The scuttlebutt on the shuttle was that a group of people who had vehicles unaffected by the EMP had started a convoy that moved from city to city around the country. The timetables tended to be unpredictable, and sometimes the routes varied based on the needs of the drivers, but as it was the only way to get anywhere faster than horseback, people were willing to wait.

Payment was difficult. Money was worthless. If you were attractive to the driver, you might be able to trade sex for transportation, but if you didn't want to go that route, you had to bring food or fresh water. Some drivers would accept precious gems or gold, which were more comfortable to carry. You could run up a tab, but that could be brutal. If the driver came looking for you and you didn't have what he wanted, you might find yourself without a vital internal organ or even your life.

Where the fuel came from the trio did not know, but Glen knew the United States government had been stockpiling fuel for years. Anyone who knew the location of those caches would have a lifetime supply of fuel, and a very lucrative business.

Glen had spent some time wondering what the government was actually up to. What did the president do with his time, stuck wherever he had been when the EMP struck? If he had been flying, then he was dead, and someone else had stepped in. But what were they doing? Working to get the power grid up and running? Chasing the disenfranchised away from the gates of the White House? Had they raided the Smithsonian for the old ham radios? In the end, it didn't matter. It hadn't affected his life, and it wasn't likely to do so. Who knew how many years it would take to get even a skeleton infrastructure running?

"What's your best guess on the days they'd pick up at the closest shuttle stop?" Glen asked. "When should we leave?"

"It's a crapshoot," Christian said. "Whenever we're ready, I guess."

"Can you three be ready to leave at dawn?" Glen asked.

They nodded, but Glen couldn't help noticing that Sally looked particularly glum. She was torn, he thought, wanting to stay and needing to go. He hoped she'd think it was worth it when it was all over.

That evening, after dinner, while they were all packing and getting the cabin ready to be shut up, Glen heard the girls talking.

"You don't have to come with me," Mia was saying. "Stay here. Glen will let you live in the cabin."

"I can't," Sally said. "You're the only family I have now. I mean, yeah, I like Anthony, but that's not a sure thing. We've barely known each other."

"Hooking up moves a lot faster now," Mia said. "You gotta go for it, Sal. Stay and see what happens. You'll be safer here than in the city."

"I'd be alone here unless I moved to the town. And then

I'd be an outsider. No, I'm going. I'm just not going to pretend to be happy about it."

Glen wondered if he should talk to the girl. Was there anything he could say that would make her feel better? Probably not. He'd better leave Sally to work through this on her own. Nobody liked a busybody.

He wondered where that saying originated? Where had he heard it? His mother most likely. The second he thought of her he felt guilty. She had been alive when he'd disappeared into the backwoods of Michigan. He'd never even said goodbye. She had been frail, and he had been afraid that telling her what he was planning would have sent her into a decline. Chances were she was dead by now. Which was both a good and bad thing.

He packed a few belongings into his small pack, placing the medical kit on the bottom. It was by far the most substantial thing he was bringing. It was the one thing he thought he would need most in the city, and possibly while getting there as well. On top of that, he placed a clean set of clothes and what toiletries he still had. He wondered briefly what it might be like to live near a big box store or warehouse. You could wander over and get those things you felt you needed. Civilization still would be available until someone raided it and took the good stuff away. And someone would, he had no doubt.

He set his bag by the door, surprised to see three backpacks bulging with things that were both heavy and obsolete. He was going to have to do something about that. He went to the sliding glass door and looked out. Christian and Mia were sitting side by side on the deck, feet dangling over the pond. Sally was wandering along the bank upstream, singing under her breath. She did that when she was nervous. He knew and felt sorry for her.

"Oy! Children," he said and waited until they all turned to

look at him. "You need to come in and repack. Your bags are too heavy to carry, and will attract thieves." He turned and went back through the door. They followed a moment later.

"We're not children, you know," Mia said. "We're all over twenty-one."

"Yes, but oy, 'Adults!', doesn't have the same ring to it, does it?" he asked with a smile. "I suppose I could say 'young adults,' or 'adults in training,' or 'people--"

"Fine," Mia said, laughing. "We'll come up with a name for you to call us. What about a family name. Like, oy, Browns? That would work, wouldn't it? And then you wouldn't have to identify us by a physical attribute. And it still would work ten years from now."

"Okay then. Let me know when you come up with a name," he said, all the time wondering if they'd all be together in ten years. Hell, they might not be alive in ten years.

He picked up Mia's pack and pointed to a saucepan dangling from a strap. "What do you think you are going to be doing with this?" he asked.

"Boiling water, heating soup, bashing people over the head," Mia said. "What would you do with it?"

"Leave it behind. I've got travel bread in the oven." He set the pack down, opened it up and pulled out three novels. "And these?" he asked.

"My favorite books," Mia said sadly. "You don't want me to leave my favorite books?"

"They'll be safe here, and there are probably still books in the city. The thing most likely to happen to books on the road is that they'll get used to start fires. Let someone else bring the fire starters." He set the pack down.

"I want the three of you to go through your packs. Pretend you'll only be gone three days. Then take out anything you wouldn't take on a three-day trip. Also take out any cooking utensils, unusable tech items you think might work in the city, and entertainment items. Remove and leave anything that is purely sentimental."

He opened Christian's pack and removed two heavy knives. "Are you an expert knife fighter, Christian?" Glen asked.

The boy shook his head.

"Then these stay behind. Someone will kill you for these, and probably with them. Unless you are intimately acquainted with your weapon of choice, leave it behind. You'll be a lot safer if people think you are harmless." He handed the pack to Christian. "Deconstruct."

Glen went for Sally's pack, but she grabbed it and pulled it into the great room. "I can manage on my own," she said over her shoulder, sitting on the couch and sorting her stuff into two piles, and then putting the much smaller, lighter pile back into her pack. "What if we need cold weather gear?" she asked.

"They have coats in the city," Glen said. "If you don't need it right now, don't bring it. You're only asking for it to be stolen from you."

Half an hour later the three packs were sitting by the front door, significantly lighter. Glen had pulled the bread from the oven and left it on the counter to cool, putting out the fire heating the oven by closing the damper and cutting off the air supply. He'd check it in the morning to make sure there were no embers left to start an unattended fire.

"I'm heading for bed," Glen said. "It could be a while before we get a good night's sleep, so I suggest you do the same."

Sally's head popped up from the armchair where she'd been sleeping since they arrived. She'd made herself a nest there with the ottoman and curled up like a dog. "I'm already in bed," she said, cheerful for the first time that day. "Goodnight!"

Mia and Christian were out on the deck, watching the stars. "We'll be in soon," Mia said when Glen poked his head out the door. "We know we are getting up at dawn."

"Goodnight, then," Glen said, and he heard their replies as he slid the door closed. He went out the front door to spend a few minutes looking at his stars without disturbing the lovebirds. He'd have to climb to the roof of a building to see the stars in the city, he thought. He pushed away the sadness. This was his decision, after all. No one was making him move to the city.

He stood a few minutes, meditating on the beauty of the stars before going back inside. He followed his familiar bedtime routine and laid in his familiar, comfortable bed. He was a doctor, and he owed it to himself to practice his craft, but the leaving wasn't easy.

CHAPTER THREE

INSTEAD OF TAKING their usual path down into the valley and toward New Town, Glen went to the old pickup in the driveway, reattached the distributor cap, and cranked it over. It had just enough fuel to get them to where they were going. If they had the pick-up point wrong, they'd either have to beg for gas or walk. But Glen thought they might as well use it. It was unlikely they'd be back, and even if he did make it back again, the battery would be dead, the tires flat and the oil congealed. This was one last trip for the old truck.

The back roads close to the cabin were free of vehicles, for the most part, but the closer they got to the freeways the more vehicles had been abandoned on the road, their electronics fried by the EMP. Many of the cars had been shoved to the side of the road, and while they had to weave around the occasional Olds Cutlass that had run out of gas, the majority of the vehicles were late model electrics or hybrids.

After a while, Glen realized he could spot the differences between the cars that had been here since the initial blast, and those that had been abandoned more recently. There were newer vehicles than he'd imagined there would be. How many people were parking vehicles underground or in Faraday cages? He began to wonder if cars parked in lots under apartment or office buildings had been protected from the effects of the EMP.

He had so many questions that he began wishing he had brought the crank-operated ham radio with him. He'd put money on the radio operators knowing the answers to most of his questions, *and* the location of the shuttle stop. He hit his forehead with the palm of his hand, and all three of the trio turned their heads to look at him, eyebrows raised.

"I just realized we could have used the ham radio to pinpoint the location of the shuttle," he said. "I don't know why I didn't think of it before now."

"You mean this ham radio?" Sally said, lifting a canvas bag that was hidden beneath the trio's feet. "I thought it might come in handy."

Glen laughed. "How did you even know what that was?" he asked.

"I was snooping around, looking for things that might be useful," she said. "I didn't tell you about it because I was afraid you'd think its bulk would outweigh its usefulness." She elbowed Mia in the ribs. "Did you see what I did there?"

"We all saw," Mia said, sarcasm dripping from her voice.

"When we stop for the night we can check on the location," Sally said.

"Yes, we can," Glen agreed, pleased that Sally had taken the initiative. That radio would be a valuable tool.

As the day wound down, Christian started looking concerned. "Seems to me like we are headed in the wrong direction," he said. "Isn't Detroit that direction?" He pointed over Glen's shoulder in the direction of the rear driver side fender.

"There are two reasons we aren't headed that way," Glen said. "One, there aren't any shuttle stops in that direction.

Two, we don't have enough fuel to get to Detroit. On top of that, Eric tells me that driving into the city as a single vehicle is dangerous. One of the reasons the shuttle was started was the idea of safety in numbers. So, we're going past our destination for the right reasons."

"Oh. Okay," Christian said. "It just seemed odd to pass the turnoff. Are you sure we don't have enough gas?"

"Doesn't matter," Glen said. "Eric was certain, and I trust his instincts. If he says it's not safe for us to drive into the city, then it's not safe. I'm not risking your lives for expediency."

"And I, for one, appreciate that," Mia piped up. "Eric and Anthony know a lot about how things work now. I feel safer knowing that we're doing what they suggest."

"It's not that I don't trust them," Christian said, sounding irritated, "it's just that I wanted to know why we weren't heading directly for the city, that's all."

The old truck started clunking and stuttering not too long after that and Glen pulled off the road, parking behind a school bus that had been abandoned. Sally pulled down the tailgate and set up the ham radio, cranking the handle to give it a charge.

"You know how these things work, Glen," she said. "Why don't you teach me?"

Glen showed her how to use the radio, and then sent out a CQ, saying CQ three times and then, "This is Glen Carter."

"This is ARC One," came over the radio. "What can I do you for?"

"We are looking for the shuttle going into Detroit. We're about a day out to the southwest." Glen put the mic down, waiting. "This could take a while," he said.

But it wasn't that long until ARC One was back online. The shuttle stop was to the south, a three-hour walk, and was expected tomorrow. Glen thanked ARC One and signed off.

"That's how you use the radio," he said to Sally. "And I'm grateful you brought it."

Sally made short work of packing the radio back up and slinging it on her back over her backpack. Glen offered to carry it, but Sally felt she should carry it as she was the one who brought it. Glen thought he'd give her an hour and then offer again. He knew from experience that the radio could get heavy after a while. It wasn't one of the new lightweight models, but a hand-me-down, an old army model with some bulk. Glen was sure the first soldier who got to switch from this model to a newer lighter model had done some celebrating.

They walked down the center of the southbound interstate, the trio in front with Glen following a few paces behind.

"You know what we are missing?" Sally asked. "Zombies. Every post-apocalyptic movie I've ever seen has had zombies in it. I keep expecting to see them come streaming out of the distance."

"Oh, no," Mia said. "You will not be giving me nightmares. No more talk of zombies."

"Not even that zombie movie where they start getting better at the end?" Christian asked. "You never could resist a movie with a happy ending."

"Oh yeah, recovering zombies. Such a happy ending, how could I resist?" Mia said.

"We should dress up as zombies when we get to Detroit." Sally took on the stumbling gait of the undead. "Scare those city people half to death."

"Get ourselves killed, more likely," Christian said, doing his own version of the zombie shuffle. "Get our heads knocked off with baseball bats."

"Can't we just talk about how beautiful a day it is?" Mia

asked. "Or where we're going to stay in the city? We probably should get that sorted out."

"We had an apartment in the city," Mia said. "We could go there, I still have the key." She fished around in the little messenger bag that she kept on her person almost all the time and dug out a key on a feathered key ring. The feathers were looking tattered and the worse for wear. "See? Here it is."

"It's a place to start," Glen said. He knew it was very possible someone else was living there by now. Or it could have been looted and left uninhabitable. But it wouldn't hurt to check it out.

He thought about the home he had left behind in Philadelphia. Who lived in it now? A bunch of squatters, or a family sticking together for safety? He thought of his cabin with more regret even than his house. The cabin had been his home for a long time. It had housed him during one of the worst periods of his life. It was a safe space, and he hated to leave it behind. But this was the right thing to do, he thought. It felt right. If you weren't part of the solution, then you were part of the problem.

"Hey, what's that?" Christian asked. He pointed to what looked like a gathering of people on a hill up ahead.

They were unnaturally still, a tableau on the hilltop, and very strange.

"I thought you said there were no such things as zombies," Sally said, her voice quavering.

Glen stopped and dug out his binoculars from his pack. He looked through them and laughed. "They are scarecrows," he said. "Someone has a sense of humor. The whole top of the hill is covered with them." He handed the binoculars to Sally. "Here, take a look."

"Oh, gross," Sally said, handing the binoculars back. "Fake blood and everything."

Christian took a look through the binoculars and laughed. "That's pretty good," he said. "Pretty realistic, considering they are stuffed with straw."

"I especially like how they've used mannequin heads and painted them," Glen said. "Someone has excellent artistic skills."

Christian handed the binoculars to Mia.

"I'm with Sally," she said. "Gross. Too realistic for me. Although, also funny in a way. You're right, Glen, someone has a sense of humor. It's heartening to see that someone had time to create such a display."

As they drew closer and could see the scarecrows in more detail, it became apparent they had been arranged to look like a mob about to stream over the hill and disrupt, or end, a traveler's life. The individuals were lifelike enough to give Glen the willies.

Could there be a person hidden in the crowd? He shook his head. There were no real scarecrows, but these were lifelike enough to give him the willies. He wondered who put them there, who had wanted to warn people off? Or were they an invitation rather than a warning? Look at us, we have it so much together that we can make jokes, Glen thought to himself He shook his head. Who knew what was going through the minds of the creators when they made this, but he admired them for it.

They passed by the hill, feeling the eyes of the zombie scarecrows on their backs as they walked away. It was kind of creepy, knowing they were back there, poised to come after them and eat their brains.

Glen knew this was fanciful, but he turned and took another look as they walked away and around a curve that would take them out of sight. An interesting psychological phenomenon, Glen thought, a group of statues that put you in fear of your life. A lot of bad had come with the EMP, but at least zombies weren't part of it. He kept thinking of them, even after they were long past the zombie-covered hill.

They passed a woman and a young boy in a field and it made him think of his wife and son. Would Clarence be that age now, his head just under Sarah's chin? No, not that tall yet. He was dreaming of them less now, and he thought it was because he had Christian, Sally, and Mia to occupy his time. He didn't want to forget Clarence. He would remember him always. He almost resented the lessening of the pain he felt when he thought of his boy and his wife, but at the same time, there still were people to live for and things to be done.

He hoped he'd be able to perform some good in the world. Something that would make his family proud of him.

Sally had started to limp. So, when Glen spotted a large rock they could sit on, he called a halt. He had her pull off her hiking boot and examined the blister developing on her heel.

"These boots are all broken in," Glen said, "they shouldn't be giving you blisters."

"I'm not the one who broke them in," Sally said. "One of the girls in town, Eliza, gave them to me. They were her sister's, and they're the right size, but obviously, they're rubbing. I didn't bring any other shoes. So, I'll just have to deal with it until we get to the city."

"You didn't bring any other shoes?" Christian couldn't keep the exasperation out of his voice. "You're wearing a pair of boots you've never worn before, and you didn't think to bring other shoes?" he repeated.

"Glen told us to lighten our bags, and two pairs of shoes isn't strictly a necessity," Sally said. "And I have worn these boots before, just not for this long."

"I'd give you mine, but they'd be too small," Mia said. "But maybe there will be someone else on the shuttle who'd be willing to trade."

"It won't matter on the shuttle," Sally said, "because I won't be walking. Just slap a Band-Aid on there, and I'll be fine. It can't be more than another hour."

Glen pulled out the first aid box and put a dressing on the blister and some moleskin around that. With luck, it wouldn't get infected. He watched her pull her boot back on, wincing. He'd have to keep an eye on her. She had a tendency to underplay her injuries, and it would be unfortunate to come up lame so early in their journey.

It was an hour and a half later when they arrived at the pick-up point. Sally was limping badly, and her mouth was set in a thin line. Glen wondered if she'd developed other blisters and thought the answer was probably yes. But he'd wait to look at her feet until they had some semblance of privacy. No point in embarrassing her further.

A small tent city had sprung up at the shuttle stop, an old rest stop parking lot. Many of the people were waiting for the shuttle, but many more were permanent residents. There was a building where you could barter goods. A woman was renting out tents like a roadside motel. She called out to them, "Want to rent a tent, love? It could be days before the shuttle comes."

Glen told her they had nothing to pay with and moved on. It was like a frontier town, only with tents. You could buy a bath, a meal, a drink, and probably sex. He'd just thought it surprising he hadn't seen any prostitutes when a young man and woman sidled up to Christian and asked him what his pleasure was.

"I don't have anything to barter," Christian said curtly, and put his arm around Mia. They drifted away. It seemed no one was going to pester you if you couldn't pay.

Not long afterward he spotted children approaching strangers, asking for food. This was something he hadn't seen in a long time. Not since he'd spent time in Mexico lecturing at a seminar. The children there had been ubiquitous. It got to the point where you didn't even notice them trying to put their hands in your pockets. He had kept his pockets empty ever since, so he plowed on through the crowd.

"Keep an eye on your belongings," he said, "Children will clean your pockets if you aren't careful. Don't let them near you if you can help it." No point in telling them not to carry things in their pockets, it was too late for that now. They chased off the children with stern faces and gruff voices and went to sit in a grassy patch near the trading post.

The trading post itself was the old rest stop building. Not a vast highway complex with fast food and a gas station, but one of the smaller buildings that would have held vending machines and free coffee, along with restrooms. The sound of a flushing toilet came from inside, and the girls looked at one another and grinned.

"I wonder if there is running water?" Mia asked.

"Let's go find out." Sally was already on her feet, her blisters forgotten with the prospect of clean hands and face.

They were back in fifteen minutes with damp faces, wiping their hands on their pants.

"We didn't want to pay for a towel," Mia said. "But it's great in there. There's a river out back and a waterwheel. The waterwheel pumps water up onto a big tank on the roof, and gravity feeds it back down again."

"I wanted to ask where the wastewater went," Sally said, "but then I decided that I probably didn't want to know. I'm glad we're not traveling downriver."

"I was thinking," Christian said, "if the shuttle doesn't come before nightfall, do you want to rent a tent? I've got a necklace I could trade."

"That's not a necklace from my mom's jewelry box, is it?" Sally asked.

"No, of course not," Christian said. "I didn't steal from your parents."

Glen cut in before a full-fledged argument broke out. "No. Save your stuff. It's a mild enough night, and we can keep watch in shifts. If we rent a tent, then we'll become a target. People with no way to pay can't rent tents. Christian, why don't you come with me to see the waterwheel."

Christian followed him into the rest stop-come-trading post, and they looked out the back window at the water-powered system. It really was ingenious.

"I'm going to clean up some," Glen said. "But before I do that, I think the girls are a little touchy about things that link them to the past, and I don't blame them for it. I would think twice about speaking openly about items you may have stolen after you joined up with the girls. I'm not saying they're fragile, in some ways they are more resilient than you or I, but certain topics set them off. I'd rather avoid internal conflicts. Okay?"

"Sure," Christian said. "You think there is going to be conflict in the city, don't you? Gangs and street people?"

"I wouldn't be surprised," Glen said. "In fact, it would surprise me if there weren't gangs and street people. I think you'll find that humans can be worse than zombies when they revert to pack mentality. Back in New Town, there were plenty of resources, but in the city, there will be pockets of people who have food and shelter and even bigger pockets of people who don't. We will have to stay alert all the time."

Christian nodded thoughtfully. "Yes, boss. Will we tell the girls?"

"Yes," Glen nodded. "But not until we are almost at the city."

CHAPTER FOUR

Melvin Foles squatted next to a corpse on the sidewalk and shook his head. He'd seen the old woman into the next life, but had he been able to obtain the medicine she needed. She could have lived many more years. The infection she died from was easily treated with antibiotics. Even out here on the street, she would have survived.

He pulled the body to the edge of the sidewalk and rolled her into the gutter. The night men would come soon and take her away. Where the corpses went, he did not want to know. He just knew that if you put them in the gutter, they'd be gone by morning. And he thanked the night men for that. If not for them, the city would be teaming with rotting corpses.

"Melvin!"

He looked up to see a tall black man striding down the street. "Joe," Melvin held out his hand to the man and then shook, touched shoulders, and broke apart.

"Melvin, you've got to get out of here, man. This ain't no place for you. You looking to get killed?" He looked down on Melvin, but just slightly. It was the bulk of the man that intimidated Melvin. Joe was all bulk, but fit, not soft. He reminded Melvin a little of The Rock, Dwayne Johnson from back in the day. The kind of man who feared nothing and no one.

Melvin was tall, although not as tall as Joe, and rangy. Thin and wiry, with long, greasy black hair. He wore it short when he was in medical school. Back then, short back and sides were the sign of a serious student. A man headed for big things. Now he was too lazy to cut it. Not that he could, there wasn't anyone cutting hair anymore, and if he did it himself, he'd look even shaggier than he did already. There really was no point.

Joe was bald, and at the moment he was thoughtfully rubbing one palm over his head. "Man," he said, "you will get yourself killed. This here is black territory."

"I'll leave just as soon as you show me a black doctor out here trying to heal the sick." Melvin crossed his arms. "I'm waiting." He looked at his nonexistent watch. "No?" he said. "Well then, I'll just get back to it, shall I?"

"Come on, Melvin," Joe said. "If you aren't out of here before dark, someone going to come out here and pop you one. Then who's going to cure us?"

"I'll be off the street before daylight fades," Melvin said, sighing. He used to say dark. He'd be in before dark, but it was dark all the time now. Even the sunniest days failed to illuminate the streets, and it was rarely sunny. Cloud cover had descended, and who knew when it would lift again? He looked up. The sky was lighter than the city around him, so it still was daytime.

"Listen, man," Joe said, "my brother got himself cut up. Can you come over and take a look at him on your way out of the hood?"

"Knife fight?" Melvin asked. "He's going to get himself killed. One of those knife wounds gets infected, and we'll lose him. There've been no shipments of meds in more than three weeks. I get notice that they've left the warehouse, but they never get here."

"It's that damn Cut Court," Joe said, lowering his voice. "They're waylaying the shipments on the way into the city and keeping all the medicine for themselves. Someone should take them out."

Melvin let his voice drop too. "The Koupe Tribinal? I wouldn't be surprised. Don't you be thinking about taking that group on, Joe. That's a guaranteed end to life."

He made his way north along the avenue, checking in doorways for signs of habitation. Tomorrow, when it was lighter, if it was lighter, he corrected himself, he'd brave the interior of some of the buildings. There would be more sickness in there than out here, and he may not have antibiotics, but there were ways of alleviating suffering and promoting healing that didn't require medicines.

Joe fell into step beside him, and Melvin smiled. He had his own bodyguard. Joe often followed him through the darker places in the city, keeping the worst of humanity at bay. Melvin appreciated the assistance almost as much as he appreciated the company.

"The man who cut my brother?" Joe said.

"Yeah, what about him?" Melvin asked.

"He disappeared. The word on the street is that the Cut Court got him." Joe dropped his voice when he said the word 'court.'

"That's a good thing then, yes? He won't be cutting your brother again." Melvin had little patience with the posturing and blade waving that went on. There was so much the people could be doing to rebuild the city. So they didn't have electricity, so what? That was no reason to slide into barbarianism.

Melvin knelt to talk to an older man in a doorway, offering

him clean water and a package of crackers. The man took them gratefully.

"Are you well, brah?" Melvin asked, using the language of the street. Or, more specifically, the slang of this community.

"I'm worried about my brother," Joe said.

"We are on the way there now, Joe," Melvin said. "I'm sure he'll be fine."

"You misunderstand," Joe said. "I'm worried the Court will come looking for him. They took one man, why not the other?"

"I see your point." Melvin thought a moment. "Well then, tell everyone he died. There's no point in coming after a dead man."

"But then the other man will be tried for killing Daniel. My lie would get him killed," Joe said.

"Let's get him healed first," Melvin said, "then we'll worry about keeping him from the Koupe. Okay?"

"First things first. Okay, Melvin, but don't you let them kill our Daniel." Joe gave Melvin the side eye, which Melvin could only just see in the dark.

"Don't you go cursing me with the evil eye, or I'll leave Daniel to rot." Melvin raised an eyebrow at Joe.

Joe had the grace to blush. "Yeah, okay. No curse."

Joe let Melvin through the lobby of an office building and up many, many flights of stairs.

"Why couldn't you live closer to the first floor?" Melvin asked. "And why an office building? Wouldn't an apartment be more comfortable?"

"The higher the floor, the less likely someone will come looking," Joe said. "Although it almost killed Daniel getting up here after he had been cut. And the night people are less likely to look for people living in work areas. These buildings have everything you need. We have a rainwater collection system on the roof that gravity feeds water to our apartment. The toilets work better the higher you go up. Stuff like that. And we got these huge windows. We can see what's happening down on the street."

"Like looking at ants," Melvin muttered. "What floor are we on now?"

"Fifteen, only seven more to go."

Melvin refrained from commenting. Although he thought a good number of things, he had to save his breath for the climb.

Daniel, when they finally found him on the couch in an office abandoned by a CEO, was in bad shape. He was sliced on the face, forearm and across his back. The cut on his face penetrated through to the inside of his mouth, which gaped when he talked. Not that he spoke much. He appeared to be high on some kind of narcotic.

"What did you give him?" Melvin asked Joe, once he got his breath back.

"Found some oxycontin in one of the offices," Joe said. "Gave him a few."

More than a few, if Melvin was any judge, but at least Daniel wasn't feeling any pain.

"Is there a first aid kit here somewhere?" Melvin asked.

Joe left, and Melvin assumed he was fetching the first aid kit. He fished in his coat pocket for his suture kit. At one time it would have held actual medical supplies, but he'd been reduced to using a sewing needle and dental floss to stitch up people. He tried not to think about it too much because that was a hole he may never get out of.

He cleaned Daniel's face and began stitching the gash, being extra careful in the area where the knife had penetrated into his mouth. Daniel groaned, but didn't thrash or try to bat his hands away, so Melvin just kept stitching. He didn't feel any satisfaction when he was finished. The man would have a horrific scar on his face, and that was if the healing went well. God only knew how he'd look if it got infected.

Melvin moved on to the other gashes, cleaning them up and sewing the edges together. He was tempted to use a blanket stitch so the scars would be more interesting, but Daniel was too far gone to give him permission. He wasn't going to further deface the man without his consent.

Joe had not returned, and it was time for Melvin to get out of this neighborhood. He jotted some instructions on a pad of notepaper. That was one advantage to an office, there always would be plenty of paper and pens. He tried impressing upon Joe the importance of finding him if infection set in, but some things didn't necessarily come across on paper. A sense of urgency was one of them.

Before he left he boiled some water over the camp stove Joe had set up in the staff room. He pulled two thermoses from his pack and filled them, saving half the pan for Joe and Daniel. He looked in at Daniel, who was sleeping fitfully. What Melvin wouldn't give for some penicillin or even moldy bread.

Back out on the street, Melvin walked quickly out of the business district and toward the East Side. He hadn't walked more than three blocks when he saw a woman sitting on a stoop in the dark. She was ragged and shivering.

"Do you have a cup?" he asked.

She nodded and pulled a chipped ceramic mug out of her bag. It had a picture of a dog on it, and Melvin wondered if it had been her dog. He didn't ask her. He'd learned the hard way that asking personal question could get you punched, or cried on, sworn at, the reactions were as varied as the number of people. He was curious and he wanted to connect, but not enough to get a mug cracked over his head.

He took the mug, opened a packet of dried soup into it and added hot water from his thermos. He stirred it with the eraser end of a pencil he'd lifted from Joe's dwelling and handed it to her.

"Be careful, it's hot."

She nodded and took the mug from him without speaking. This wasn't unusual. Many of the street people had stopped talking after time, but there was another contingent as well. Those whose voice boxes had been removed by the council, The Koupe Tribunal, so they couldn't tell what, and who, they'd seen there.

Melvin supposed he should be happy that the Court wasn't killing everyone who was hauled there against their will, but having your voice box cut out, well, that was brutal. He wasn't sure why they took the voice box rather than the tongue, but either way, it was barbaric.

He moved on, walking in the direction of home but, taking detours where needed. He handed out more soup, and cleaned cuts and scrapes. He dragged bodies to the curb. It was work that needed to be done, and he was able to do it, so he did. Cleaning up Detroit and feeding her citizens.

He made sure to pass the hospital on his way. It was tragic, but most of the people who went there were turned away. And Melvin would find them on the street outside, crying and wailing over their injured children or spouses. You had to have something of value to be admitted by an actual institute of healing, and most people had nothing to offer. He would help them in whatever way he could.

A woman standing on the sidewalk outside the hospital was holding a child, looking in through the big revolving door. The child really was too big to be carried, but she held him unwaveringly. They both were crying, the boy sobbing, and the woman with tears silently sliding down her cheeks.

Melvin stopped a few feet from her, far enough away that she wouldn't be spooked, but close enough that they could speak.

"Can I help?" he asked quietly.

"He's hurt," she said. Her voice was rough from crying.

"And what's wrong with him?" He gave her a small reassuring smile. At least he hoped it was reassuring, he'd feel awful if someone told him it was actually creepy.

"He fell, and his arm isn't working properly," she said. She nodded at the hospital doors, "They won't see him."

"No, hospitals don't help common people anymore," Melvin said. "They are all about helping themselves."

She nodded, her face looking sad. "What can I do? Will he heal right if no one will see him? Or will he end up all bent and crippled?"

"I can't say, but if you let me help you, I may be able to set his arm." It looked pretty bad just hanging there, but who knew? It may not be as bad as it looked.

"Do we have to go far?" she asked. She seemed unwilling to move from the hospital doors.

"We'll go in there," he said, pointing at the doors in front of him. The generator must have come on because the waiting area had started to glow with warmth. "They aren't using the reception area for anything."

He led them in through the doors, past the resentful-looking receptionist and over to the couch across from a coffee table. He had her lay the boy on the table and folded his own coat to slide under his head. Melvin sat on the couch next to the boy.

"What's your name?" he asked the boy while he carefully straightened the boy's arm. The fracture was apparent. Although the bone hadn't broken through the muscle and skin, the forearm was a misshapen lump, visible at the site of the break.

"Grady," the boy said, the waver of fear in his voice.

"Well, Grady," Melvin said, "this is going to hurt. We want

your arm to grow straight so you'll be able to toss a ball with your buddies, so I need to set it. Okay?"

The boy nodded, his eyes wide with fear.

Melvin turned to his mother. "Go sit by Grady's head and hold his good hand steady. If you have something he can bite down on, that's even better."

The woman reached down and tore some material from the hem of her tattered dress. She wadded it into a ball and offered it to the boy.

"Go ahead," Melvin said. "Bite down on that, it will make it better."

He examined the boy's arm, calculating exactly how much force he would have to use to set the bone, and then he turned to the mother again.

"Talk to him. Tell him a story that will distract him or ask him questions he has to think about the answers to. Grady, are you ready?"

The boy nodded, and the mother started talking. Melvin grabbed the arm with both hands, pulled the break apart and carefully set the bones together again. Grady called out in pain once, and then it was over.

"Good job, Grady. Good job, Mom." Melvin felt relief wash over him. That could have gone very wrong but didn't. He fished a disposable coffee cup from his bag and made the boy some soup. He wasn't done yet, but he wanted to administer some pain pills, and that wasn't wise on an empty stomach.

"I still need to splint this," Melvin said. "But I want you to drink this first. Okay?"

Grady nodded and took the cup, sipping the warm liquid. The mom turned away.

"Are you hungry?" Melvin asked. "I've only got one cup, but I'll make you some when Grady's finished."

She nodded. "Thank you," she said quietly. "I didn't know what to do. Or what I would have to do."

He nodded but didn't say anything. He knew what she meant, what service she might have to offer to get her boy treated by anyone but Melvin himself, but he wouldn't embarrass her by saying so.

"I still need to splint Grady's arm," Melvin told her. "And I want to give him something for the pain, but he needs to finish his soup first."

"All done," Grady said lifting the cup in the air. "Your turn, Mom."

Melvin took the cup and made soup for the woman. Then he poured some hot water into the lid of the thermos so it could cool. He got up. "You two stay here," he said, "I need to find some things."

He wandered past the reception area and into the hallway toward what used to be the emergency room. Maybe it still was the emergency department, he didn't know for sure. No one stopped him, but he could see guards posted at the stairs. He nodded at them as he went by. The emergency department was deserted. Apparently, only the rich had emergencies that actually got treated in a hospital, and only on the upper floors.

That suited Melvin just fine. He found the room where casts used to be applied to broken limbs and started searching. The place had been looted, the drawers and cupboard doors left open, and while there was plenty of trash in the form of packaging, there was little that was useful.

In a drawer he found enough cotton batting to wrap a child's arm and in a cupboard enough ends of casting tape to go over the batting. He even saw stockinette, lots of it. Maybe looters didn't think the thin bandages were worth stealing. Melvin loaded his pockets with the things he needed and strolled back down past the guards, nodding as he passed them and on into the lobby.

Grady and his mom still were there. He wasn't surprised, but then he wouldn't have been surprised if they had left either. Melvin tested the temperature of the water in the thermos lid. It was drinkable. He fished the casting supplies out of his pockets and then rooted around for a bottle of painkillers.

He cut a pill in quarters and gave one to Grady and the cup of warm water. The others he gave to the mom. "One quarter every four hours," he said and watched her slide them into her own pocket.

He busied himself setting out the supplies, keeping a surreptitious eye on Grady to be sure he swallowed the medicine. Then he sat back down on the couch and had Grady sit on the edge of the table. "Hold your arm like this," Melvin said, demonstrating with his own arm.

Grady complied, and Melvin got to work sliding the stockinette over the arm, up over the elbow to the armpit, being careful not to bump the area with the break. He smoothed the light fabric so there weren't any wrinkles, and then began wrapping the cotton batting, adjusting the position of the boy's arm.

The casting material he put on looser than he might have before the EMP blast. The arm might swell, and no one would be there to remove it. On the other hand, he didn't want the child to reinjure his forearm because the cast wasn't tight enough. It was a tricky balance.

When he was done, the arm was wrapped in black, blue, red, day glow green and yellow, which seemed to please Grady. Of course, he didn't know that he was lucky to have a cast at all. Materials were harder and harder to find. Even scraps were being scavenged by people like him. The good stuff was being hoarded by people like the ones upstairs.

Skilled and privileged, wanting for nothing, and giving nothing away. Melvin despised them.

He had Grady sit where he was, and he went hunting again. He only needed a scrap of material and was eyeing a privacy curtain in one of the rooms when he noticed a stack of pillowcases that had been knocked to the floor on the far side of a bed. He grabbed them and returned to his patient.

He used two of the pillowcases to make slings for the boy, ripping them into strips. One he tied around the child's neck and arm, adjusting it so there weren't any pressure points. Melvin had had a lousy experience with pressure points before the world went wonky. One of his nerves had not recovered, and he suffered from tingling on occasion.

The other sling he gave to the boy's mother so she'd have a spare if needed. She looked tired, her eyes dull and heavy, barely responsive.

"Let me carry him home for you," he said. "I know he's old enough to walk, but I also know that you aren't going to let him. So let me. You show me the way, and I'll leave you a couple of blocks from your home if you like, so you don't have to worry about me showing up unexpectedly." And asking for sex, he didn't say out loud.

She agreed and led him out of the hospital and in the general direction of her own neighborhood. She tripped on a rough spot on the sidewalk, and he caught her elbow to steady her. She gave him a small smile, and he shifted Grady so he could carry the boy with one arm and keep his other hand on her arm. She was so tired that he thought if she was alone, if she didn't have the responsibility of the child, she would have sunk to the sidewalk and slept there.

He was surprised when she turned and walked toward a small apartment complex. The kind that has two stories with ten or twelve apartments surrounding a small courtyard. But she walked steadily through the common area and out the back, where there were storage sheds for the tenants to use. She led him to the furthest one, tucked in the corner of a paved parking area surrounded by a chain-link fence.

He left them at the door to the shed, where she was fumbling with the lock. When he turned back to make sure they were safe before leaving they had disappeared inside and pulled the door closed. It was only then that he realized he never had asked her name.

He hurried away. There were several blocks to go before he arrived in his own neighborhood, and it was long past dark. He strode quickly, not paying much attention to the buildings he was passing, except to watch for marauders on the street. They could be hiding between buildings or in doorways, so he walked in the middle of the street to give himself some notice. It was as dark as the deepest mine. At least that's how it felt to Melvin. There was a hint of light where the road crossed a drainage ditch, and he looked down. A family was huddled around a fire built in a small ring of rocks near the entrance to the drain pipe.

He turned aside, climbing down the embankment to approach them.

They huddled together when they noticed him, the parents shooing the children behind. They knew the drill, the smallest stood between their parents and the older children for safety.

Melvin raised his hands, palms out to show he meant no harm, but they didn't relax their guard. So many families had been torn apart, wives and children sold into slavery, the men killed or sent to work for the current powers that be. It was brutal.

"Excuse me," he said, "but it isn't safe to camp here. That is an active storm drain, and it doesn't take much rain to fill it. You'll drown if you stay here."

The mother sighed audibly, but the father protested.

"There's no rain expected tonight," he said. "I have a friend who reads the weather."

"That may be true," Melvin replied, "but rain isn't the only condition that will fill the drain." They looked miserable. They were sniffling, with red noses, and the younger children had mucus crusting their nostrils. All eyes were on him, and they were red-rimmed and watering, every last one. He rummaged in his pack and brought out the remainder of his packets of dried soup. "Do you have a way to heat water?" he asked.

They fetched a pan. Melvin poured the last of his hot water into it, and they added water from their stash. The mother produced a grate and laid it across the top of the garbage can where the fire was burning.

While the water was heating, Melvin went back into his pack and pulled out a tattered ziplock bag full of gummy vitamins. He handed them out, making the adults take them as well as the children. He gave the remainder to the mother, "Everyone gets one every day until they run out. Okay?"

"Yes." She nodded tiredly. "Thank you." She produced a variety of cups and bowls, and when the soup was hot, Melvin helped her pour it out. He refused any for himself and sat on a rock to watch them eat while he decided what to do about them.

One of the corpses he had rolled to the curb today had been a man he'd recognized. He'd lived in an apartment building not far from the one where Melvin had lived. If they acted now, they might be able to commandeer it before anyone else did. It seemed like the ideal situation if you weren't the dead man. He waited patiently while they sipped their soup, the youngest draining their cups quickly and asking for more. He obliged until all that was left were a few short noodles stuck to the sides of the pan, and those were gobbled up by a boy. He ran his finger around the edges of the pan, sucking the remnants from his finger.

"I know a better place for you to stay," he said once everyone had settled down. "It'll keep you out of the weather, and if you are careful about never leaving it empty, you could stay there indefinitely. And you won't be in danger of being swept out into the lake by a storm surge. Do you want to see it?"

They did want to see it. The group gathered their belongings, which didn't take long, and followed Melvin up the embankment onto the street. They walked huddled together down the dark avenue, Melvin leading them. They were skittish in the dark, the children especially seeing things that weren't there, but finally, they arrived at a modern apartment building.

They went in through the parking garage, where a door to a stairwell was propped open with a spare tire. They trudged up five floors, and Melvin led them to the door he believed belonged to a now-empty abode.

He knocked, and there was no answer. No one yelled for him to go away or that they had a firearm and were ready to shoot. So, he pushed the door open. What had once been a lovely midrange apartment with three bedrooms and two baths now looked like it had been ransacked. And it was possible that had been, but it was also possible that the open drawers and toppled furniture were camouflage. There was no point in sacking a room that already had been rifled through. So, if you gave the impression that a place already had been gone through, you had more of a chance of retaining your belongings.

The homeless family surged in, making noises of appreciation. While the children claimed bedrooms and discussed whether they could flush the toilets, Melvin showed the mother and father how the door had been modified to include not just an extra deadbolt but also a two-by-four slid into brackets on either side of the door frame.

"When I leave," he said, "you must lock all the locks and bar the door. Someone should stay in all the time with the door secure. If you do that, then you can stay indefinitely."

"How do you know the owner won't come home?"

"Because I rolled him into the gutter this morning," Melvin said. "Just good timing I guess."

They thanked him, and he left, finally heading for his own home.

CHAPTER FIVE

GLEN GROANED when he and Christian left the building and discovered Mia and Sally surrounded by a group of women. A dark-haired woman had their attention, the girls' faces reflecting their surprise and horror.

"Damn," Glen said. "We shouldn't have left them alone."

"Why?" Christian asked. "What's up?"

"Because that woman is telling the girls horror stories about the city," Glen said. "I'd put money on it."

They approached the group, and Glen smiled, "what's up?"

Sally looked up at him, confusion and anger on her face. "Did you know that there are gangs in the city?" she asked. "People die on the street, and their bodies are rolled to the gutter to be picked up during the night? They don't even know what happens to the dead." She looked shocked and distressed, along with the anger and confusion. "Why are you taking us into that?"

"Maybe we should talk in private," Glen said. "I really don't feel the need to explain myself to people I've never been introduced to."

The women began getting up. "Sorry, didn't mean to intrude," an older woman said. "We wish you all the luck in the world. I understand you are attempting to do good, and I hope you are able to accomplish that goal." She nodded her gray-haired head to him and led the others away.

"Well?" Sally was standing, hands on hips.

Glen looked down at Mia. "You aren't upset?" he asked.

"No, I had a good idea of what we'd be getting into, but I couldn't see staying in New Town just keeping our little group safe. People need help in the cities. Someone has to help restore order. Why not us?" She sat back against the tree. "But that's just me."

Glen switched his attention back to Sally. "Yes," he said calmly, "I knew there was likely to be danger, and I was planning on telling you once we got closer to the city. I didn't want you to be worrying the entire trip. I'm sorry if it seems as if I was withholding information from you. Traveling is so much better if you're having an enjoyable time. I didn't want to ruin that for you."

Sally deflated. "I guess that makes sense," she said. "But I might have stayed with Anthony had I known. That wouldn't have been so bad."

"You are right," Glen said, "I should have been more specific about the kind of danger you might be getting into. I apologize."

"Don't," Christian said. "We all know what the city is like. We came from there. We'd just forgotten how bad things were."

"And that things probably were getting worse, not better," Sally said sadly. "A big city doesn't recover as quickly as a small town, does it?"

The shuttle, when it arrived, was like something from a Mad Max movie. Whereas Glen had envisioned an airport parking lot shuttle, the vehicles that pulled into the rest area were a mismatched assortment of owner-modified vans, cars, motorcycles, pickups and one truck-trailer pulling an old school bus with the windows boarded over and a platform welded onto the back where four men with firearms sat.

The school bus doors opened, and an assortment of people as mismatched as the vehicles streamed out. They disappeared into the trading post as quickly as they had appeared. Passengers also disembarked from the vans, but these people were cleaner, more relaxed. Glen realized these were the comparatively wealthy, those who could pay to ride in relative comfort.

The driver of the semi jumped down from his cab and started calling for travelers to the city to gather round. He was like a circus barker, yelling "Roll up! Roll up, now, folks! I've got something to say."

When Glen finished listening to the driver he went back to tell the others that the shuttle wouldn't be departing until morning since it wasn't safe to arrive in the city after dark.

"We'll need to set watch," Glen said. "As long as one of us is awake to scare the bad guys away we should be fine."

"But no tent?" Christian asked. "I feel kind of vulnerable sleeping out here in the open."

"The trouble with a tent," Glen said, "is that you can't see them sneaking up on you until it's too late. It would take a lot of bodies to surround us out here."

"I see your point," Christian said, but his expression told another story.

"Mia," Glen said, "you take first watch. It's the easiest, then me, then Christian, and then Sally for the last."

"Why do I get the easiest?" Mia was affronted by his lack of confidence in her.

"Because you and Sally are the most vulnerable. You are the smallest of us, and most likely to attract attention, but if there are other people still awake and watching, you'll be less likely to become a target."

Mia didn't look happy, but agreed to take first shift. It was only two hours. She settled herself with her back against a tree and Glen sat against a nearby tree and let his chin drop to his chest. Not a great way to rest, but if someone approached he'd be awake and alert at a moment's notice.

Glen awoke and knew something had gone wrong. His internal clock told him that Mia should have woken him by now, and when he looked for her, she was nowhere to be found. Christian was snoring gently, but Sally was not in her bedroll.

"Christian, wake up!" Glen barked.

The boy was startled awake and sat up. "What?" he said, looking around sleepily.

"The girls are gone." Glen tried to keep the panic from his voice. "We need to find them."

"Are you sure they aren't in the ladies room?" Christian asked. "You know about women and bathrooms."

"Mia wouldn't have left her post without telling me," Glen said. "Get out of that sleeping bag and put your shoes on."

While Christian was struggling out of his bed and into his shoes, Glen gathered up the most important of their belongings. He noticed the radio had gone missing along with the women, and he wondered how the thieves had known about it. Of course, Mia and Sally probably showed it to the other women who'd approached them today. They would have trusted a kind older woman. No one's grandma was a robber.

When Christian was ready, Glen led him back to where the tent rentals were. He leered at an older woman sitting outside and asked, "Where would I find a little company, love?"

She directed him around the back of the clump of rental tents, to what must have been an old maintenance building.

Another older woman was sitting in a plastic chair outside the door, and Glen recognized her as one of the women who had been talking with Sally and Mia earlier that day. He didn't stop to chat, but went right past her and yanked the door open.

"You can't do that!" the old woman yelled, but Glen and Christian ignored her.

The inside of the building had been partitioned into makeshift rooms. Glen slammed open the first door, but the woman inside wasn't Mia or Sally. "Where are my friends?" he shouted, but the woman just cowered, so he moved on. Christian, taking his lead, took the left side of the corridor, while Glen took the right. The old woman was pulling at their arms and shouting at them, telling them they had no right and to get out. Glen turned and glared at her.

"Either you tell me where my friends are, or I will open every single door in this building," he said. "And if I do not find them, I will beat every person in this building until someone tells me where they are. So, either cooperate or get out of my way."

The woman shrunk back against the wall and Glen opened yet another door to yet another woman who wasn't either of his friends. They kept moving, but the woman had begun to speak, and now she was grabbing at Glen's arm so he would listen to her.

"I'll show you," she said. "They have not been harmed. I will show you where they are. Just stop this." She did not look defeated, but rather like a woman who knew that you don't win every hand, and perhaps this was the time to fold gracefully.

She led them around the corner and up a metal staircase to the second floor. There she opened the door into a room lined with bunk beds. Sally and Mia were both out cold on mattresses on the far side of the room.

"What have you done with them? Or rather, what did you give them?" Glen asked. He'd seen enough drugged patients to know these two were not just sleeping.

"Just a mild sedative," the old woman said. "It will wear off soon. I have a man waiting for that one," she said, pointing at Sally. "I'll offer you a good price for her." She grinned and her mouth was full of rotten teeth. Glen winced.

"Don't sell my friends," he said. "And while you're at it, I want my ham radio back as well."

"What radio?" she asked, but then she saw the look in his eyes and nodded. "I will get you the radio."

While the woman was out of the room, Glen and Christian went to the girls. Glen checked respiration and pulse, relieved to find them healthy. He picked up Sally, and she groaned as he placed her arm over and down his left shoulder bringing her body across his shoulders. At the same time he placed her one leg over his other shoulder, motioning Christian to do the same with Mia. Then they turned and went in search of the old lady and their radio.

She might have tried to escape, but it seems she was smarter than that and was waiting at the outer door with his radio, still in its case, in her hands.

"I think you should be more careful about friends you try to abduct," Glen said. "One of these days you'll choose a woman who knows how to fight, and you get yourself killed. Why not stick with women who are willing? At least then you'll have the moral high ground."

She didn't respond, so Glen shrugged, took his radio and headed back to their spot under the trees. Surprisingly, their bedrolls and few belongings still were there when they got back. Perhaps the old woman had the monopoly on thievery in this particular location. They laid the women on their bedrolls and Sally began to moan.

"I have such a headache," she said, rubbing her eyes.

"What happened? Oh, wait, I remember some crusty old man wanted to have sex with me, but he couldn't because I was losing consciousness. I'm so glad that old hag drew the line at letting him rape me when I was out. How's Mia?"

"Still unconscious," Christian said. "I'll bet she's pissed off this happened on her watch."

Glen nodded. "And I'd like to know how they were able to abduct her before she gave the warning. They must have been silent."

"Silent as the grave," Sally said. And then, when she saw Christian and Glen looking at her, added, "It's from a Jane Austen movie," she said.

Christians snorted and knelt down next to Mia, rubbing her arms.

"I'm sorry," Sally said, "but not everything is guns and cars, as much as you guys would like it to be."

They might have argued that point but Mia had begun groaning and thrashing around. "Let me go!" she said, and Christian yanked his hands away. But she opened her eyes and smiled. "You're not the old bag. Lucky for you, I was about ready to take a swing at you."

"How did she get hold of you in the first place?" Glen asked.

"I was stupid," she said dejectedly. "She stood over there and beckoned me. I thought she needed my help, but instead held some foul-smelling cloth over my face. If this were an historical novel, it would have been ether or some sort of spirits. Next thing I knew, I was in a room with a bunch of other women standing in front of this group of men. It's pretty clear what we were there for, so I started swinging. Not that that did me any good. They just drugged me again. It's a good thing you came to rescue us because I might've killed somebody if you hadn't." She sat up leaned to the far side of her sleeping bag and vomited in the grass.

The next thing Glen knew, Sally was vomiting too. Christian started to turn green, and Glen sent him to fetch water. "Don't come back until you don't feel sick anymore, you understand?"

Christian nodded and hurried away.

Glen grumbled about being left to clean up the girls by himself, but he didn't mean it. He knew only too well that it took a particular kind of person to deal with vomit, mostly moms and nurses, but the occasional doctor was good at it too. How fortunate for him that he was one himself.

Glen kept watch for the rest of the night, knowing he probably could sleep during the ride into the city. He woke the others at dawn and they packed up, used the restrooms, and went to stand in line for the shuttle. He was tempted to offer a little extra to ride in the comfortable vans, but it was a waste of resources. So, he tamped down his annoyance and gave the man at the door a supply of sterile bandages. The driver was quite pleased.

He almost laughed at that. How fortuitous that he would possess some of the most valuable items in today's world. Had he known he would have stored more medical supplies. He was feeling a bit antsy. It had been a very long time since he'd been in the crush of humanity and he was low on sleep.

It was dark inside the bus, the windows being covered in plywood that was bolted to the metal body, and the only light coming through the dirty windshield. The bus was towed by the cab of a semi and the windshield wasn't really needed. Glen was a little surprised they hadn't covered that as well, but glad they hadn't. Without the front windows, they might as well be riding in a shipping container with seats bolted to its floor.

They took seats toward the back of the bus where there was a bit more room. Mia curled up and put her head on Christian's shoulder, the pair of them dropping into unconsciousness almost immediately. Sally took a double seat and curled up, Glen couldn't tell if she was sleeping or just lost in her own thoughts. At some point, they would have to talk about what had happened last night. Too bad he wasn't a psychologist. If he had been, he'd know how to help her. He took a seat in the back and leaned against the cool glass of the boarded-up window and slept.

CHAPTER SIX

MIA AWOKE with her senses on high alert. The rocking motion of the bus had stopped, although she still could hear the growl of the semi's engine. They weren't moving, and not being able to see out the window made her feel claustrophobic. The words to a David Bowie song her mother used to sing ran through her head, *"For here am I, sitting in a tin can..."* But instead of being far above the world she was stuck on its surface.

She took deep breaths through her nose, forcing down the panic that threatened to overtake her. *Here I am sitting in a tin can. A sitting duck. Trapped.* The fear began to well up again. *Breathe, Mia, breathe.* She looked around. Christian and Sally still were asleep, but Glen was alert and had the look of a man who was listening intently.

She slid out of the seat and went to the front of the bus to peer out the windshield. There wasn't much to see. The cab of the semi towing them blocked the forward view, and nothing was happening on either side. She stepped down into the stairwell and put her eye to the gap between two boards.

One of the outriders was sitting on his motorcycle just outside the door. Guarding them, she thought.

He was facing the rear of the bus, and it seemed as though that's where the activity was. He had one hand on the gun in his hip holster, the other on the bike's accelerator. She could hear the low whine of the engine and see the vibration even at an idle. It occurred to her they were sitting ducks. There was only one way in and out, the emergency exits had been boarded over. *Here we are, sitting in a tin can*.

She pushed open the door and stepped down out of the bus into the late morning sunshine. The shuttle was stopped in the middle of the interstate; a bus had been rolled across the road, blocking the lanes. Behind the shuttle a series of off-road vehicles had pulled to a stop, preventing escape in that direction. Mia marveled at the variety of machines that had made it through the EMP, from off-road motorcycles to ATVs to four-wheel drive trucks. There had to be at least twenty-five vehicles out there. Each with at least one driver, some with passengers as well.

Two people, possibly a man and a woman, stood forward of the pack talking with the driver of the semi towing the bus. Mia hoped someone else on their team could drive the semi. Otherwise, if something happened to the driver they were stuck. The pair carried weapons held ready in their hands, pointed at the ground, but just a finger twitch away from lethal.

The men on the platform on the back of the bus held their rifles loosely by their sides, almost casually, unless you noticed their set jaws and the tension in their necks. They all were standing, except for one woman who sat on the edge of the platform, legs crossed at the ankles, swinging her feet. She projected an image of a summer's day picnic by the lake. But she not only had her rifle out, but also a handgun tucked into her waistband and a knife in a sheath on her thigh.

The guy on the motorcycle guarding the bus noticed Mia. "Get back on the bus," he said. "I can't protect you if you are out here."

Mia wondered if he could protect her at all. She went back on the bus to talk to the others.

Everyone was awake now. "What's going on?" a man called from the middle of the bus.

"It looks like a hold-up," Mia said. "But I don't know for sure. A man is guarding the bus, and he said we should stay inside so he can protect us."

She moved to the back of the bus, ignoring the questions peppering her. They could just work it out for themselves.

"I'm not comfortable being trapped in this bus," she said as she flopped into her seat next to Christian. She'd almost said "trapped in this tin can," but she felt the further she got from that song the better. Dragging dreams into reality was not a good thing.

"I understand it's easier to protect one entrance, but there's no escape if it's breached. And what's to stop those highwaymen from just opening fire from outside? This bus isn't bulletproof." She looked around at the plywood-covered windows and wondered if the glass would shatter in on them when the bullets came through the wood.

"We are an investment," Glen said. "If we go missing or are injured, word will get out that the shuttle isn't safe. It's probably at least partially why we're boarded in. We can't see the scary stuff. They put us in a box and protect it. We get to where we're going none the wiser and spread our happy message that the shuttle is safe and wonderful, if hot and stuffy."

"I don't like it," Christian said. "I think we should go out and join the fight. I don't need to be protected."

"I'm not sure they need more people," Mia said. "There are several vehicles and about twenty riders between them and us. But I wouldn't be adverse to escaping this death trap and catching the shuttle again up the road."

"They might not pick us up again," Sally said, "and we'd have to walk to the city. Well, or get picked off by the bandits that apparently roam the highway. I'm glad we didn't see them on our way to the shuttle stop." She shivered. "I didn't realize the roads weren't safe."

"We were probably safe enough," Glen said soothingly. "It's not like we were carrying boxes of loot or anything like that. Had they approached us I would have given them the radio. It's the only thing we have of value." His look told them not to mention the jewelry each of them had hidden on their person. That was something they did not need to advertise. There were probably passengers inside the shuttle who were just as ruthless as the bandits outside.

Mia looked around, assessing the other passengers. Anyone of them could be listening, and their encounter with the madam at the shuttle stop had taught her that little old ladies were not necessarily kindly personages wanting to help. She couldn't really trust anyone outside their small group.

"I want to step outside for some air," she said, "and maybe freshen up some." She gathered her bag under cover of her last sentence and started off the bus, hoping the others would get the hint and follow.

"Wait up," Sally said, "I'm coming too."

"You shouldn't get off the bus, girls," a middle-aged woman with tired eyes said from near the front of the bus. "They can't protect you if you get off the bus." She didn't try to stop them as they passed, however. So, not a guard in disguise.

"Come on, Glen," Christian said. "We might as well go too. There may not be another chance before we get to the city."

No one else followed, which relieved Mia but also worried

her. Was everyone else in on the holdup, or were they just too smart or too scared to leave the perceived safety of the vehicle? The guard on the motorcycle outside just shook his head at them. Mia almost could hear him thinking 'there's one in every crowd.' Only in their case, it was four.

They skirted around the front of the bus, clambering over the tow-bar. As they passed the big truck cab, Mia looked up. The driver side door wasn't closed all the way. "Anybody know how to drive a tractor-trailer? she asked. All their heads were indicating no. They didn't know how to drive a tractor-trailer, and why would they? "Should we hide in there then?"

"I don't think so," Glen said. "It's too coincidental and too close to the bus." His eyes widened, and he grabbed Mia, pulling her away from the truck.

She whirled to see the barrel of a gun poking through the slightly open door. Behind that, she could see a pair of eyes staring her down. The contrast between the dark inside of the truck and the bright world outside made it hard to say what color those eyes might be, but Mia's imagination supplied steely-gray, and that seemed appropriate.

"Get back to the bus." The words from inside the semi were thick with gravel, like she'd smoked too many cigarettes and wasted her voice box.

Mia wanted to reply 'Make us!' but she'd become a little more circumspect and possibly a little more mature, to say nothing of wanting to stay alive. She and Glen began to back away, and she motioned to Christian and Sally to get moving away from the semi in the opposite direction from the bus. Mia darted around the front of the semi, out of the line of sight. She hoped the shooter wasn't stupid enough to discharge her firearm through the windshield, but it wasn't Mia's fault if she did.

They jogged away, winding their way around and between the shuttle vehicles and cars that had been abandoned on the freeway. The lead vehicle had a cow catcher on the front, and Mia wondered if this was how they'd cleared the first path through all the cars and trucks. From the looks of it, it had been rush hour when this area had been hit by the EMP. There was almost a solid wall of cars along the side of the roadway.

So they kept moving, winding in and out of the lead vehicles and the cars that had been abandoned on the road. The drivers of the shuttle vehicles ignored them, if they saw the four of them at all. Their attention was focused on the scene playing out behind them.

When they reached the bus that had been pushed across the road, Mia noticed there were tire tracks worn into the ground behind the bus. This bus was moved frequently, it seemed. She followed the ruts to a concrete slab hidden behind weedy bushes. Perhaps this was a 'regular' stop on the shuttle run, and the standoff a performance the passengers never got to see. Or maybe the guy on the motorcycle was correct, and there was one in every crowd, the intended audience of the tableau.

Mia turned to Glen. "Are you thinking what I'm thinking?" she asked.

"If you think the hold-up is a regular performance put on for the benefit of the travelers on board the shuttle, then yes, I'm thinking what you're thinking," Glen said grimly.

"What are you talking about?" Christian said, narrowing his eyes.

Mia showed him the tire tracks behind the bus and the concrete slab where it rested when not used as a roadblock.

"What's it called when you are pressured for money you've already paid?" Sally's mouth was drawn into a thin line.

"Highway robbery," Christian said.

"Extortion," Mia said.

"A shakedown," Glen added.

"What are we going to do about it?" Sally asked.

"Walk to Detroit," Glen said. "I doubt they'll pick us up again without another payment. And I'm not paying."

"Maybe one of these cars is old enough that it didn't have any electronics to get fried," Sally said, motioning to the cars lining the interstate. "Someone could have been stuck in a gridlock of non-functioning cars. You never know."

"Keep an eye out," Glen said, "but don't be disappointed if they've all had their fuel siphoned out. They've been here a long time, and I have a hard time believing no one thought of stripping them of every useful item, starting with the gasoline."

"Why hasn't word gotten out about the shuttle people shaking down its passengers?" Sally asked, skirting around a dirty white Prius. "You'd think that would be common knowledge by now."

Mia ran a finger across the hood of an old Honda. There was a thick layer of dirt covering the cars, and she wondered if the rain washed them clean or just made them muddy. If they did find an old car to drive, they'd have a hard time getting the windshield clean.

"Maybe it is common knowledge, and we just weren't in the loop," Christian said. "Maybe everyone else on the bus had been through that before and had their little cache of valuables all ready to be handed over."

"As if," Sally said. "Here I thought, 'How altruistic to run a shuttle so people can travel,' when in fact, it's just another way to rip off people." Her face reflected the disgust she was feeling. "I can't help but look for the good in the world, but it's sure not easy to find."

Sally clumped along in front of Mia, muttering to herself and smacking the hoods of the cars they passed. Mia felt for her. This was not the world they were expecting to inherit from their families. Not that she'd been anticipating a bed of roses, mind you. Her family had worked hard for what they had.

It struck her that maybe she wasn't smart to be returning to the city. A lot of bad things had happened there, and she suspected there were more to come. Evil, too, probably. She was going back because she didn't want to be separated from Christian. He was her lifeline in this world. But was he going to be able to protect her? They had barely made it out alive the first time.

She began seriously doubting what they were doing. Glen felt the need to do good in the world, but he could have been helpful in New Town. The city was a wild place, where you could lose your life in a moment of inattentiveness. Only instead of lions, the predators were human, and they weren't interested in killing you for food. They took pleasure in the pain of others, both physical and mental. Death could take days to catch up with you.

Mia felt the bile rising in her throat, and she pulled in deep breaths of air through her nose. She didn't want the others to see how afraid she actually was. Her own thoughts were scaring her more than the women in the brothel had done the night before. She probably would have been safer in the brothel than she was out here.

She noticed Christian watching her, and she smiled, pretending again. It was the only way she'd make it through. Just keep pretending that everything is okay. We aren't walking to our deaths, no, we are traveling to where we are most needed. Yes. She used that as her mantra, 'we are going where we are needed.' It was calming, as long as she didn't think about the fact that she wasn't needed at all. It was Glen whose skills were required, and she had no clue as to why she, Sally, and Christian were tagging along.

Lambs to the slaughter, that's what they were.

She shook her head. That wasn't it. We are going where

we are needed. She only wished the image in her head didn't depict them as sheep and Glen as their shepherd.

Lambs to the slaughter, going where they were needed. Ugh.

They heard the shuttle long before they could see it. The rumble and whine of engines grew louder. They stepped to the side of the road when the dust trail became visible. It was surprising just how dusty the freeway had become. Now it was like watching a convoy streaming across the desert, the dust blowing up on both sides of the road.

They blew on by without even slowing, the dust choking the travelers on the road. The driver of the semi pulling the bus waved as they went by, but the travelers flipped them the bird. Disappointment flooded through Mia, settling as a lump in her stomach as the vehicles rushed by. They weren't even going to try bargaining with us, she thought. Her motorcycle rider raised two fingers in greeting as he went by, but he was wearing his helmet with the visor down so she couldn't see his expression. They probably left travelers by the side of the road all the time. Nothing for him to regret.

But the last van before the rear guard pulled over, and the side door slid open. A gray-haired woman put her head out. "Get in quick," she said and moved out of the way. They didn't hesitate and climbed in, crawling forward to let the others in. The door slid shut, and they were moving again to a chorus of horns sounding behind them.

"We aren't supposed to stop," the woman said, "but I bartered a lot of goods to have this van to myself, and if I want to pick up people, I damn well will."

The woman wasn't old, but her eyes were lined, and fine wrinkles were accentuating her laugh lines. Her hair waved in silver strands around her face and Mia could see that it was otherwise black. Her eyes were bright and alive, and her expression intelligent, and Mia suddenly no longer was afraid.

If this woman was going to the city, then perhaps Mia would survive after all.

The woman held out her hand to Mia, but instead of a handshake, she clasped Mia's hand in a two-handed embrace that was warm and comforting. After she'd clasped the others' hands as well, she nodded and smiled.

"I am Anna Marie," she said, "and my driver tells me her name is Speed, which I'm inclined to believe." The woman behind the wheel looked into the rearview mirror and nodded before focusing back on the road ahead.

There was no passenger seat in the front, but what looked like a cooler with a box of weapons balanced on top of it. The back was empty of seats as well, being taken up with a mattress and pillows, as well as smaller beanbag-like chairs. Mia realized the van had been set up to hold as many people as possible. It was much easier to pack people onto a mattress than into bench seats.

And yet there was a lone passenger, someone willing to pay a premium to ride alone. She wondered why. Surely it would be more prudent to share with a fellow traveler or two.

Anna Marie was watching her face and seemed to know what she was wondering. "Even a gentile-looking woman can rob you in your sleep," she said. "I prefer to pay up front and know that my throat won't be slit and my body dumped in a ditch. Not everyone has the means to safeguard themselves in that way, but I do."

"We set watch," Sally said. She'd been watching Anna Marie watch me, Mia thought. "That's how we stay safe."

"Thank you, Anna Marie, for stopping," Glen said. "I greatly appreciate not spending the next three nights sleeping near the road."

"You paid for passage," she said. "I saw you board the bus at the shuttle stop. I feel people should get what they pay for."

"But what if we rob you and leave your body in a ditch?" Mia asked.

"But you will not." Anna Marie smiled. "For one, I have no need of sleep before we reach the city, so you would not be able to take me unaware. For two, should you try, Speed would kill you. She is not only my driver but also my bodyguard for the duration of this journey. And third, I would not have picked you up if you were the type of people to rob an old lady making a pilgrimage to her hometown."

"You are not an old woman," Christian said. "I'm pretty sure you could take on all four of us, even without Speed to back you up."

"What gives you that idea?" Sally asked.

"I don't know," Christian frowned. "But I'd be surprised to find out anyone had taken Anna Marie unaware. Do you have psychic abilities?"

"As far as I know, no one has psychic abilities. However, I am a keen observer and a student of body language and motivations, as well as human behavior. I don't let down my guard, but I also don't let anyone near me whose motivations aren't clear to me."

"I'd ask what my motivations are," Mia said, "but I'm not sure I want to be that self-aware."

Anna Marie laughed. "Very wise, young Mia, you are very wise indeed."

"How long has it been since you've been in Detroit?" Glen asked Anna Marie. "And why the pilgrimage? Surely it isn't the same city you left."

"I was twenty years old when I left Detroit," Anna Marie admitted. "So, it is most definitely not the same as it was then, even if the world had not ended. But I have memories that haunt me, so I must go back. And there are wrongs done that must be redressed if I am to go on with my life. And so, the pilgrimage. Why are you headed into the city?"

"I have a specific skill that I haven't been sharing with the world for a few years now. I hear it's needed and I feel compelled to help." Glen shrugged. "It's as simple as that, really."

"May I ask what skill it is you possess?" Anna Marie said, lifting her eyebrows.

"I'm a neurosurgeon, or at least I was in another life."

"That is a skill in need." Anna Marie said to him, without asking why he hadn't been practicing it. "And your traveling companions? Why are they headed to the city?"

"Glen's never been to Detroit, and we came from there," Sally said. "We're his guides."

"All three of you?" This time only one eyebrow lifted.

"We are a team, a family," Mia said. "Where one goes, we all go. We watch each other's backs."

"I see." Anna Marie smiled grimly. "I suppose that is less expensive than hiring bodyguards and paying for vans. But then I can afford to travel alone. I left my companions where they would be safe."

"And they let you go?" Mia asked. She couldn't imagine letting Glen or Christian go off on their own. After all, that was why she was here.

"I left them a note," Anna Marie said. "If I'm lucky, they'll only just have read it by the time I get back. I'm usually lucky," she added, as if an afterthought.

Mia could believe it. Anyone who could afford to pay for a driver/bodyguard and van also could buy their own luck. "Where are you coming from?"

"California. The Sacramento Valley?" Anna Marie's eyebrow raised again.

"I've heard of the Central Valley, of course," Mia said. "But I've never been there."

"I did my undergraduate work at UC Davis," Glen said. "I'm intimately acquainted with a number of bars in Sacramento. Or at least bars that used to be in Sacramento. Don't know if any of them are still there. Are bars still a thing? Can anyone get alcohol?"

"Sure," Anna Marie said. "Some places are hiring brewmasters or vintners to supply their customers. They get food and housing and all the beer or wine they can drink. I don't know what they do for incidentals, but then I don't know what anyone does for those. I pay good money -- well, what passes for money -- to a woman who procures goods for me. I know I'm one of the fortunate few. The one percent still is able to live comfortably, as long as not all their fortunes were in banks."

"That must be nice," Mia said. "But we've been very comfortable in our little town. Well, we don't actually live in the town, but are associated with it. We take care of Glen, he takes care of the town, and the town takes care of us."

"A sound arrangement," Anna Marie said. "I only wonder why you would leave."

"There is a greater need for me in the cities," Glen said. "That's where people go when they need a specialist. But from what I've heard, unless you're rich you can't get treated. I want to change that, at least for neurosurgery."

"You'll have a hard time finding a sterile environment outside of the hospitals," Anna Marie said. "You may not be able to accomplish everything that you would like."

"That is the risk," Glen said, "but if I don't take the risk, nothing will change for certain."

"Indeed." Anna Marie pointed out the windshield. "You just about can see the city now."

The four craned their necks to catch glimpses of Detroit, but this far out all they could see was a generic skyline of tall buildings reaching into the air. The downtown area didn't seem to be much larger than a city like Sacramento, and a handful of skyscrapers broke up the horizon, but that was all.

"Where did you say you were from, Glen?" Mia asked. "Philadelphia? How different is it from Detroit?"

"Philadelphia is bigger, has more tall buildings, and is sandwiched between two rivers. Detroit has the Great Lakes and a river and a smaller downtown area," Glen said. "I believe they are culturally different as well. Detroit has Motown, although I don't know how it might have changed since the EMP. Philadelphia has the Philharmonic, and tends to lean toward being classier, or at least more stuck-up."

Anna Marie laughed. "I think you'll find Detroit is just as stuck-up, but about less cultured things. Or, to be more politically correct, differently cultured things. How do you compare the Philharmonic with Motown? You just can't," she said. "But the good people of Detroit are just as proud of Motown as the people of Philadelphia are of the Philharmonic. Perhaps Philadelphians dress up more often, or used to, when dressing up was an option. But that also could be just my perception."

"You don't need electricity for music," Sally said, "so why wouldn't there still be concerts?"

"It's just not safe to go out in large numbers," Anna Marie said. "If there are musical gatherings, they are likely held in private homes behind iron gates."

"Or on back porches in the neighborhoods," Mia said. "Let's not forgot music is available to everyone. Not everyone can afford a violin, but most of us are born with a voice."

"Although some of us are also born tone-deaf," Christian said, "and you're asked not to sing."

"It's been a long time since I've heard live music, or recorded music for that matter," Sally said. "I hope we find some here, because I really miss it."

Christian looked at her in surprise. "I didn't know that about you," he said. "Do you play an instrument?"

"Piano," Sally responded, "but quite badly. And that was before I stopped practicing."

Mia laughed. "Don't listen to her," she said. "She plays very well in a range of musical styles. If we're fortunate enough to find a piano, we could make her play, and that would be all the music you'd ever need."

"Don't exaggerate," Sally said. "And anyway, any piano we are likely to find is going to be way out of tune."

Mia shrugged, and let the subject drop. If they did find a piano, Sally's fingers would tell the story that she now was trying to ignore. Fifteen years of piano lessons did not produce a mediocre player, no matter what Sally said.

"And where will you be staying in the city?" Anna Marie asked.

"My family kept an apartment here," Mia said. "If it hasn't been taken over by squatters, then we will stay there."

"And if it has been taken over by squatters?" Anna Marie asked.

Mia just shrugged. Who really knew the answer to that?

Anna Marie rifled in the back and came out with a piece of paper and a pen. She wrote on it and handed the paper to Glen. "If you find yourself without a place to stay, come find me," she said. "I've got plenty of room, and you'd be welcome."

The foursome thanked her, and Glen slid the paper into his inside jacket pocket. Mia thought she saw relief flicker across his face as well as gratitude. She didn't blame him. It was always good to have a backup plan.

When the van reached the city center, they parted ways with Anna Marie. She shook each of their hands and then walked away across the street. As she stepped onto the sidewalk, a tall gentleman slid out of the afternoon shadows and joined her. They shook hands and walked away together. Mia felt a pang of anxiety for Anna Marie. She hoped she got where she was going, that the memories haunting her finally would be put to rest.

Mia took a deep breath and got her bearings. Then she said, "this way," and led the others toward where she hoped her home lay waiting.

CHAPTER SEVEN

THE SUN WAS on the rise as Melvin climbed the three flights of stairs to the apartment. He stumbled on the last fight and came down on his knee, swearing at the pain. What he wouldn't give for a working elevator at the end of a night like that one. Fatigue washed over him as he dragged his weary body down the hall to the apartment.

He carefully unlocked the deadbolt and the handle of the front door. Then he pulled a magnet from his jacket pocket and placed it precisely two inches below the top of the doorframe. He slid the magnet carefully to the right. This movement was accompanied by the welcome rasp of metal on metal. He repeated the action five inches from the floor. When he'd installed these magnetic locks, he'd had to resist the urge to place them symmetrically, each two inches from the top or bottom of the door. That is what most people would do, and it just made it easier for burglars to break in. So he didn't. If his hypothetical criminal happened to carry a magnet and happened to discover his first magnetic lock, it would at least be harder to find the second.

He sometimes wondered if he should install a third lock.

But so far he hadn't needed it. He slipped through the door and bolted the inside deadlock and the handle. He left the two bars alone. He didn't feel the need to latch them when he was at home, since he could hear if someone was trying to get in.

Inside he performed his customary security sweep, moving room to room looking for intruders. He checked the shower, the closets, and under the bed before heading to the kitchen and lighting the propane-fueled stove with a match. He'd never come home to find an intruder, and he'd stopped expecting one, but you never knew when you might come home to see the original owners settling back in. Or people who fancied themselves the new owners.

He wondered if they had escaped the city, leaving many valuable possessions behind. Or if they had been killed, enslaved, or just had died quietly by the side of the boulevard, like so many others. He'd put the family photos away in a drawer It unnerved him to have the former owners watching him from inside their frames. He felt their disapproval of him using items they'd left behind in a panic.

But they had left them, Melvin reminded himself. If they'd really wanted or needed an item, they would have taken it with them, or come back for it. And they had not. He thought he must have survivor's guilt. He was living in comfort when the people who belonged here had disappeared to no one knew where.

He ate his oatmeal quickly and then padded down the hall in his stocking feet to the master bedroom where there were Egyptian cotton sheets on the bed, and a high loft comforter spoke to him of luxury. He drew the curtains and crawled under the duvet, falling asleep as his head hit the pillow.

CHAPTER EIGHT

GLEN MARVELED at Mia's grasp of the city. She remembered the layout of the streets and walked them unerringly, winding around the dregs of humanity who appeared to be living everywhere, in one case in a tent in the middle of the street. And why not, he supposed. If the shuttle was the only car with fuel, what was the harm in setting up in the middle of a side street? Many families were living in vehicles, from city buses to mini-vans, and he couldn't help but wonder why? There must be thousands of unoccupied homes and apartments. According to his comrades in New Town, millions had died in the immediate aftermath of the EMP.

Passengers had died in vehicles that still had momentum but whose drivers had not been able to steer and had careened off the roads. People in places that relied on air being pumped to them, like miners and deepwater divers, had suffocated. Patients had died on operating tables or in hospital beds attached to machines that no longer could keep them alive. People had been trapped in airplanes that had dropped from the sky, and still more had been crushed by those same planes.

The stoplights had stopped functioning, so those cars that could be driven, such as the old Volkswagen Bug that was overturned next to a major intersection, were in danger of being hit by cross-traffic. In this case, an ancient International pickup looked to be the cause of the Bug's demise.

So, why were all these people living in the street? They smelled of body odor and disease, and he could see that Sally was trying not to wretch. No one came toward them, no one begged or asked for anything. The car dwellers stared silently, moving when necessary to get out of the foursome's way. They passed what Glen was sure were corpses in the gutter, and twice he saw bodies being dragged into the street.

Detroit had been a vibrant city, and he was sure people who had owned brightly colored clothing must still own it. However, everything was gray and brown, due to dirt and wear or on purpose he could not know. Away from the open spaces, the shadows between the buildings turned the afternoon to twilight and that further dulled the people. They watched with haunted eyes and Glen thought they were afraid. For some reason, Glen and his companions were different enough from the people of the streets to cause them to draw away.

They turned onto another street. This one once had been quietly residential, but now there were stalls on the sidewalk, an impromptu market. One pushcart was selling nothing but tortillas, plain tortillas, freshly made. A sign pinned to the cart made it clear that medical supplies, small metal items, and nonperishable foodstuffs were acceptable currency, but money was worse than useless. Try to pay a merchant with it, and you would be driven from the market.

Point taken, Glen thought. Had he any paper money he'd be tossing it in the trash about now. He was surprised that such a sign was needed. Surely anyone who'd been anywhere in the last three years knew better than to try to pass bills. They had no value except in extreme cases where a vendor had their head in the sand and was counting on the United States to step up and back its currency.

Mia stopped and parted with some of the small packets of medical supplies Eric had given her before they had departed New Town. Currency had no value anywhere, and he'd known they would need those supplies where they were going. Glen hoped she was spending wisely because those supplies were limited, and he was going to need them himself. At least until they discovered if the small amount of precious metals they carried could be converted, and that could take a while in a town where there was no one they trusted. Silver and gold had value as raw materials, but only if you knew someone who actually was producing items with it. But Mia came away with apples and bottled water, and he had to admit they needed to eat. He noticed she stayed away from the sandwich and bakery stalls, places he'd gravitate to. He'd have to ask her about that later.

He saw a woman holding a crying child going from stall to stall, asking a question. Time after time the stall operator would shake his or her head, and she would move on. He reached out and caught Mia by the shoulder. "Wait a moment," he said.

He went to stand near the woman as she asked yet another vendor for help. Her daughter's arm hurt, was there a doctor who could help? She could not afford to go to the hospital, and she was pregnant, so she could not pay the other way.

He did not pretend he didn't know what she meant. He was appalled there was no medical clinic for the public to access. He stepped closer and put his hand on her arm.

"I'll help you," he said. "For free."

She looked at him warily. "No one helps a stranger for free," she said, and turned away.

Sally appeared at her other side. "It's okay," she said. "He's a doctor, come here to help. Let him help your daughter." She reached out for the child, but the mother held on tightly. "She can sit in your lap. Look, we'll go over there and sit on the steps." She pointed to high steps leading up to what looked to be a library.

They moved to the building. Christian and Mia were holding back so not to startle the mother, but Sally sat next to her, talking quietly, soothing the woman with her voice. Glen sat on her other side, and the child looked at him with frightened brown eyes, the lashes coated with tears.

"Where does it hurt?" he asked the child.

She pointed to the arm she hugged tightly to her body.

"May I touch it?" he asked. "I want to feel the bone. Okay?"

She shook her head no with such vigor that her dark curls whipped around her head.

"Can you show me where it hurts?" Glen smiled gently. He wanted to draw the child out, but if he were too forceful or too cheerful, or too anything for that matter, he would scare her back into her shell. If she stopped communicating, they were sunk.

The child pointed to her wrist and Glen could see it was bruised and swollen. He thought about medical history and how doctors assessed a break before x-rays. Best to treat it both as sprained and broken. The young mother was going to have her work cut out for her once this child was feeling better. He reached into his backpack and pulled out an elastic bandage and a small piece of casting plaster to mold into a splint.

"Can you hold your arm out like this?" he asked the child,

demonstrating with his own arm. "I want to splint it, so it feels better."

The girl nodded and held out her arm, although her lower lip trembled.

"That's right," said Glen, "hold it just like that. If you can hold it still, I'll give you a piece of candy." He motioned for Mia to bring him one of the bottles of water she'd purchased and he dampened the plaster. Then he molded it to the lower edge of the girl's arm and pulled it away to let it harden. Plaster sometimes generated heat and he didn't want to burn her arm.

"Okay, Momma, watch me put this on," he said, holding the now-hardened plaster in place and rolling the bandage around the child's arm. The trick was to make it tight enough to support the limb without making it so restrictive that it cut off circulation. It likely was going to swell more, and as he wanted to see her again in a day or two, he wanted to make sure she wasn't going to be in pain. Reluctant patients had a way of not showing up for follow-up appointments.

"If you have to take it off, or if it becomes too loose and needs to be rewrapped, the important thing is don't wrap it too tightly. You don't want to cut off the circulation in your daughter's arm. Watch her fingers, if they become swollen or start turning purple, then loosen the bandage. Meet me back here in two days at this same time. Okay?" He observed the woman's face to see that she understood. He slid his hand into the front pocket of his backpack and pulled out a peppermint, handing it to the girl.

Her face brightened, and she snatched it from his hand, unwrapping it and popping it in her mouth before her mother could tell her no. She walked away under her own power, her uninjured hand clutching her mother's.

Glen went to get up, but before he could a man appeared and sat on the steps where the mother and child had been a moment before. The man pulled a none too clean rag from his hand, displaying a nasty wound on the fleshy part of his palm underneath his pinky finger. It was inflamed and oozing and, frankly, smelled disgusting.

"How did you do this?" Glen asked.

"Got cut on a piece of glass," the man said. He looked to be in his mid-30s, tattooed and rough-looking, as if he hadn't slept in a very long time and hadn't bathed for even longer. The smell of the wound competed with the smell of his unwashed body.

Glen had encountered worse in medical school, so he breathed through his mouth and got on with it. He rinsed the hand thoroughly and then washed it with antibacterial soap. It occurred to him that the supplies he had brought with him wouldn't last a week if he had to deal with many wounds like this one. He used the remainder of the water, rinsing the soap from the laceration.

"I can't stitch this," he said squeezing a line of antibacterial ointment into the gash, "it's too infected. Throw that disgusting rag away," he said, gesturing to the filthy piece of fabric on the stairs next to them. "Keep your wound clean. Come see me tomorrow."

A crowd had begun gathering around them, and he searched for Mia. He caught her eye and lifted the empty water bottle, then held up three fingers. He needed something to drink as well as water to treat the wounded. He hoped there wasn't some nasty microorganism in the bottled water, but for now it was all he had, so he would use it.

By the time Mia returned Glen was dealing with a teenager who'd stepped on a nail. As he worked, he mentally created a fee structure consisting of bottled water and clean dressings. It was evident personal hygiene was a problem for people living on the street. He knew that was a no-brainer, but until you encounter such situations many of the details escape you, or at least they had escaped him. If he had thought about it, he might've realized his patients would have had limited access to water and soap and toothpaste, but he hadn't thought about it.

He cleaned and dressed the teen's foot, which wasn't infected as of yet, thank goodness, and looked to see who the next patient would be. He was tired, but it was somehow exhilarating to be doing something worthwhile. Seeing patients again wasn't the effort that he thought it might be. He'd forgotten that he enjoyed healing people.

When he'd poured the last of his drinking water over a scraped knee, he looked into the crowd and made a pronouncement. "You'll have to bring your own water," he said, "and a bottle for payment. I'll die of dehydration if I keep this up."

That was all it took, the next person who approached him handed him two bottles of water as she sat down. She had severe acne and a sizeable infected pustule on her cheek, which was close enough to her eye to alarm him. He cleaned her face, drained the pustule, and treated it with antibiotic ointment. He was going to need a truckload more of that. He used one of his small adhesive bandages to cover the spot. Who knew that a little square of sterile dressing would end up being a precious commodity.

"You have to keep your face clean," he said. "See if you can find soap and use it twice a day. I want to keep an eye on this," he touched a spot on her face where the infection had been, "so come back and see me tomorrow. Okay?"

"I live in the street," she said. "So how do I keep my face clean? Where do I find soap? I'm not selling my body for soap. Food, maybe, soap, no." She looked at Glen with defiance. The group of people watching murmured in agreement.

"Listen, if you want to keep the sight in that eye, you'll keep your face clean and see me tomorrow. How you do that is up to you." He handed her back one of the bottles of water, took an empty one and squirted a small amount of liquid soap into it and handed her that as well. "That should help. I'll see you tomorrow." He mentally added water and soap to his list of precious commodities. He had a feeling that list would be a lot longer by the end of the day.

A spot of bright color caught his attention as a young child wearing a rainbow leotard and a neon pink tutu broke through the circle of adults. She looked about five or six years old, about the age where little girls pull their skirts over their heads during holiday concerts. An agitated woman wearing a nondescript gray coat and carrying a smaller version of the same burst through the crowd.

She caught the child's arm, saying, "You mustn't draw attention to yourself, put this on." She wrangled the child into the coat, covering the tutu, and buttoned it closed. "It's not safe. You don't want the bad men to get you."

She'd been speaking quietly, for the child's ears only, but they were close enough that Glen heard the exchange. How awful it must be to grow up in a society that requires drab conformity to ensure safety. He smiled at the girl as her mother dragged her away, and she smiled back and waved. It was heartbreaking.

Glen treated cuts, breaks, bruises, and minor ailments for another couple of hours and when he thought he couldn't cope with one more human interaction, Sally stepped in and told the others to come back tomorrow. There was some whining, groaning, and cries of "I just need..." with various items attached, but she shut them down and sent them away. She had more strength of character than Glen gave her credit for.

He gathered his supplies. His backpack was so much lighter than it had been when he began that he didn't know how he was going to go on treating people with no supplies.

It was dispiriting, but perhaps when he'd eaten, he'd feel better. It was easier to come up with solutions when you weren't exhausted and hungry.

The group fell in line behind Mia, with Sally ahead of him, and Christian behind. Glen thought they must be protecting him, making it easier to wind through the street people. There were cries of 'Doctor!" as he went by. News must travel fast here. He was too tired to respond, and Sally waved them away, telling them to come to the library steps tomorrow afternoon.

They followed Mia down an alleyway, and through a parking garage to a locked door. She pulled a keyring from her pocket and unlocked the door, which opened into a stairwell.

"It's only three flights," she said, and started up.

Glen counted the stairs as they climbed, eleven steps and a landing, eleven more steps and a door. Eleven steps, landing, eleven steps, door. Christian put a hand on his back and pushed him up the last flight of stairs. Glen was grateful.

They came out of the stairwell and headed down a long hallway, stopping three-quarters of the way down in front of a door with the number 42 in bronze. Mia unlocked the deadbolt and then the handle, stowing her keys back in her pocket. Glen saw her cross her fingers as she pushed open the door.

CHAPTER NINE

Mia knew the chances of her family's townhouse apartment being untouched were slim. She desperately hoped it would be, if perhaps not looted, at least not trashed. She crossed her fingers behind her back, a habit from her childhood, and pushed the door open.

At first glance, the apartment looked untouched, although all the pictures had been removed. That seemed odd, but not as strange as the sound coming from the hallway. A man appeared, wearing only boxers and socks. He was rubbing his eyes as if he'd just woken up. He was startled when he saw them standing in the doorway.

"I wondered what woke me up," he said sleepily. "I didn't know I had company."

He was unarmed and seemed surprisingly unafraid. He ran a hand through his untidied hair and stared at Mia. "Do I know you?" he asked. "You seem familiar to me."

At that moment Glen stepped between Mia and the man. His shoulders were rigid, and Mia could tell he had steeled himself for a confrontation. She stepped up next to him and put a hand on his arm.

"It's okay," she said. "This is just how things are now. And anyway, he doesn't look like much of a threat, does he?" She felt Glen relax beside her.

The sleepy man clapped a hand to his forehead. "I know!" He went to a drawer and pulled out a picture of Mia's family. "Look, it's you!"

He displayed a framed photo of a family in which Mia was front and center. "This is your apartment, isn't it?" A look of profound disappointment crossed his face. "I'm going to have to leave, aren't I?" He looked down at himself. "Well, not dressed like this, I hope. Give me a minute."

He disappeared back up the hallway. Mia and Sally looked at each other and broke into giggles. Mia didn't know who this man was, but he'd made her laugh for the first time in what seemed like ages. She dropped her backpack on the floor and sank into the couch facing the sliding glass door onto the balcony. There was nothing but two bars holding the window closed. A balcony had become a liability, apparently.

"Do we really have to turn him out?" Sally asked in a low voice. "He's so funny, and he seems harmless."

"You can't take for granted that he's harmless," Glen said. "Some people are excellent actors."

"He's right," the man said, coming back into the room. "These days you should just automatically assume that everyone is out to get you. Or at the very least out to stay alive at any cost." He reached out his hand to Glen. "Melvin Foles," he said. "I'm a medic of sorts. I've been trying to establish a regular supply line for medical goods, but it's an uphill battle."

"Medical supplies?" Glen said, his interest showing on his face. "I've only been here a few hours, and mine already are severely depleted. Can you tell me how to go about replenishing them?"

Melvin sat in a chair across from the couch. "I usually go

out about now, to see if there's anyone I can help. But it can wait. It's not like it won't all still be there."

"What do you do out there?" Mia asked. She liked this unassuming man. He was friendly in a hostile world, and yet he knew what was what. That was a good quality in an ally. She thought they should keep him as one.

"Oh, you know, I roll corpses into the gutter for pick up, hand out chicken soup and water. Sew people up when I can. I was a medic in the Middle East, and this is mostly field medicine, so I'm right at home. But supplies are deadly difficult to come by. Just when I think I've got something set up, the Koupe keep interfering. They either disrupt the roads, or they take the supplies for themselves. It's fucking frustrating."

"How do the hospitals operate?" Christian asked. "The one we passed had its lower floors burned out."

"They do that on purpose," Melvin said, grimacing. "It's easier to restrict access if you've only a couple of stairwells to guard. Trained doctors are pricey, only the very rich can afford them. Every procedure brings in profit. They live well, and therefore they have to protect themselves from the masses. I have practically nothing. I help everyone and, so far, knock on wood," he knuckled his head, "I've been left alone."

"Left alone by whom?" Sally asked. "This Koupe thing you talked about? Is that like syndicated crime or something?"

"The Koupe Tribinal, or Cut Court if you prefer the English version, is a tribunal set up by the very wealthy and powerful of the city. Needless to say, you don't want to come to their attention. If you go before them, you pretty much can count on being executed. I've never heard of anyone coming out of there alive. Syndicated crime has far more sympathy and shows more mercy than the Koupe. Hell, regular criminals do too. They, at least, are just trying to stay alive. The Koupe is amassing power. Far more dangerous, in my opinion."

"If you are doing good works, then why are they disrupting your supply lines?" Christian asked.

"Because he who controls the supplies, controls the people," Melvin said. "It's all about power and money." His stomach growled loudly, and he blushed. "I'm going to make some oats, do you want some?"

"Hell yeah," Christian said. "I'm starving." He turned to Glen. "Why didn't we make traveling bread to bring with us this time?" he asked.

"I did make it," Glen said. "We left it on the counter back at the cabin. I was so concerned with traveling light and having supplies to barter with, I forgot all about it. I hope Anthony eats it or takes it down to his workers."

"When you go back to see patients at the library tomorrow," Mia said, "take payment in food. That way at least we won't starve."

"Not a bad plan," Melvin said from the kitchen. "Wait. You were treating patients at the library? You're a doctor?" He came back in the room with five bowls of what looked like oatmeal.

Mia sighed. They'd been spoiled back at Glen's cabin. He kept a garden and went hunting, and other supplies could be bartered from the people in New Town. She had the feeling they'd be eating a lot of oatmeal here in the city.

"I'm a neurosurgeon," Glen said. "But I haven't practiced in some years. However, I can't sit by and do nothing with so many people in need, and I'm not interested in treating only those who can pay. So, that means treating people on the steps of the library, at least for now."

"A neurosurgeon? Wow. If the hospital consortium knew about you, they'd be on your tail to work for them. You could be rich." Melvin sounded slightly awed.

"I'm not interested in being rich," Glen said. "I'm interested in helping people. They can blow me if they think I'm going to treat only those who pay. On top of that, I have no desire to be associated with an organization that ignore the problems of the society they are living off of."

"You know, I think I like you," Melvin said. "What do you need for supplies to get you through tomorrow?"

Glen told him what he needed and then started on his bowl of oatmeal. Mia thought it must be cold by now, which probably wasn't a good thing. It hadn't tasted all that great warm. It was more 'oatmeal-like' than like real oatmeal. Sally and Mia gathered the bowls and carried them into the kitchen, where they wiped them out with a damp cloth that was sitting by the sink. No point in wasting water. After all, they would have to haul it up here. They left the bowls on the counter and found the drawer where the spoons belonged.

Mia noticed the silver flatware still was in the drawer and was shocked. Why hadn't Melvin used it to buy supplies? She thought she knew the answer. He was the type of man who would seek shelter in an abandoned apartment but would not steal the items that belonged there. She liked him all the more for it.

And, it meant that the valuables still were here in her family's apartment, which meant she could use them to buy food and supplies as needed. That was a relief. After today she doubted the coins and jewelry she had brought with her would be worth anything at all. Silver at least could be melted down and made into things. At least she hoped that was true.

When they moved back into the living room, Melvin was putting on his dark jacket and slinging a dirty gray-green backpack over his shoulder.

"Are you leaving?" Mia asked. "There's plenty of room here. You don't have to leave because we came."

"I'm not leaving leaving," Melvin said with a smile. "I'm

far too interested in what you all plan to do to disappear from your lives. No, I'm going on my rounds. I'll be back in the morning. Probably just as you all are leaving for the day. I've been sleeping in the first bedroom, but I don't mind sharing, especially as we probably will sleep in shifts. I make it my job to find and help the night people."

"Stay alert," Sally said. "It can't be safe out there after dark."

"I hit the most dangerous neighborhoods before the sun goes down," Melvin said, "and head back to less dangerous territory when dark falls. People almost always are hanging around the hospitals, wondering why they can't get help. It's very safe there because the hospitals are well lit and heavily guarded. They have fuel for their generators. You can't get help from them, but I know families that live on the streets that surround them, or sometimes in the old parking lots, because they feel safer there." He pulled his hood over his head. "See you in the morning."

When the door closed behind them, Mia looked at Glen and raised her eyebrows. "How could we have gotten any luckier?" she asked. "Not only is he a medic, he knows the medical supply chain. And do you know, he hasn't looted my family's silver? It's all still in the drawer in the kitchen. We can use it to buy essentials."

"I admit he does seem to be the genuine deal," Glen said. "But let's not forget, even he said we need to be careful who we trust. We'll be cautious. Even with him. Okay? Keep your personal details to yourself."

"So, what?" Christian asked. "First names only? I can't see how it matters."

"Did you notice he didn't even ask our names?" Sally said. "He told us his full name and didn't even ask ours. And he left us here without any concern for his belongings."

"He might not have any belongings," Mia said. "They

might all be mine, or at least my family's. I'm going to look in the master bedroom and see what he's left here."

The others followed her down the hall past a bathroom and a laundry alcove to the first door. "This was my parents' room," Mia said as she pushed open the door.

The bed was rumpled, and there was a towel tossed over the end of it. There was a pile of clean clothing on a chair that Mia didn't think belonged to her dad. Other than that, it looked just the same as the last time she'd been in the room.

Her mother had been sitting at the dressing table, doing her hair for some charity event. She was meeting Mia's father at the gala. Mia and her mom had been alone in the apartment. Mia had wanted to quit college, but her mother wasn't having any of it. If Mia were living under her parents' roof, then she'd need to stay in school. And if she weren't living under her parents' roof, then she'd have to work, because her mother wouldn't pay for it.

Mia had explained, begged, and wheedled to no avail. "I'm not learning anything," she wailed.

"Then you aren't taking the correct classes," her mother spat back at her. "You need to challenge yourself." She turned and looked Mia in the eyes. "You are an intelligent young woman, Amelia, and I won't have you waste that working at Walmart. You'll be happier in the long run if you get your education now.

She'd been frustrated with her mother's lack of understanding. Tears came to her eyes as she remembered the words they'd exchanged, hot and angry, no compromise on either side. She wiped the tears away, hoping the others wouldn't see them. She pointed to the pile of clothing on the chair.

"Those are Melvin's," she said and moved to the closet, opening her father's side. "These are my father's," she said, "feel free to take what you need." She pulled out a clean button-down flannel and tossed it to Glen. "That might be nice for tomorrow."

She opened a dresser drawer and pulled out pajamas for both men and handed them each a pair.

"God, this is luxury," Christian said. "Thank you." He went to the closet and shuffled through the hangers. "Melvin hasn't even touched this stuff," he said. "That's wild."

"The jeans and T-shirts are here," Mia said, pulling open the doors to the wardrobe. "Oh, and sweatshirts, scarves, gloves. You name it."

She pulled a scarf from the pile and put it against her cheek. It did not smell of her father any longer, but she pictured him wearing it the Christmas she gave it to him. He wore it all day, every day, for a week. She remembered him at the breakfast table in his pajamas and robe with the scarf wrapped around his neck. She had been ten, and yet here it was, still in his drawer after all that time. She wrapped it around her own neck and stepped back to let Glen and Christian take what they needed.

"Sally, my mom's clothes are here, but you'll probably fit better into my stuff. It's down here." She led Sally from the room, past the second door in the hall, saying, "bathroom," and opened the door after that.

This was her room, utterly untouched since she'd been in it last. Well, not wholly untouched, the cleaning lady had been in to pick up her discarded clothing from the floor and make the bed. She opened the closet and gestured to the dresser. "Take whatever you want," she said. "You can have this room. I'll bunk with Christian across the hall."

"Are you sure?" Sally asked, but Mia already was out of the room and opening the door across the hall. She stepped into the spare room, which doubled as her father's office in town.

She moved the chairs from the near side of the desk and pulled down the Murphy bed. It was entirely made up with sheets and blankets, and she went to the closet to pull the pillows from the shelf. She tossed them on the bed and flopped down, burying her face in her father's scarf. Only then did she let herself cry.

CHAPTER TEN

Petra heard the footsteps behind her and increased her speed. She kept from breaking into a run by sheer self-control. If whoever was following her realized Petra knew she was being followed, they would stop stalking and pounce. She understood the risks, and moved at a fast walk, hugging her coat around her to give the impression she was hurrying to get in from the cold.

In reality, she was sweating with fear. Her shirt clung to her back and chest, and a fine trickle of moisture ran from her hairline down her cheek. She kept her breathing regular, counting inhalations and exhalations, pushing down the sobs that threatened to erupt from her chest. Rule three: don't show fear. She'd already broken rule one and two: don't be caught on the street once the shadows have fallen, and never travel alone.

But she'd needed to get out to join her friends, who insisted on a regular social gathering in the evening, as if they still had pre-EMP twentysomething lives. The lives they'd expected to have. She'd been feeling stifled by her father's iron-fisted rules, his insistence that she couldn't keep herself safe. She'd escaped out onto the street, and she was paying for it now, proving her father right, which would have stung if she hadn't been so busy being afraid.

The dusk was falling, the footsteps closing, and her heart pounding so loudly she wasn't sure if she was misunderstanding what she was hearing. Was that a second person, or an echo of the first? She was in an area of town where she'd never been before the collapse of civilization. The buildings were old and run down, the paint chipping from the doors and window frames and the stone marked with faded graffiti. Here and there a window was broken, cracked or boarded up. She knew it didn't matter, there were no places that were safe anymore, but the dilapidated condition of the buildings increased her unease.

A light shone from a window, not candlelight, but something brighter, battery-powered at a guess, and she could see the shadow of her pursuer from the corner of her eye. She didn't dare turn her head to see the dark smudge in the shadows, and couldn't tell if he was getting closer. She was reasonably sure it was a he, not that women weren't also predators, but something about his style, his pace, his patience made her believe it was a man. And she'd better do something soon, or she'd be his prey.

She scanned the street, hoping for a family group huddled in a doorway, or signs of the party that should be close now. Nothing, no safe haven for her. Damn it, there should be some sign of the gathering by now. She took a chance and turned down a side street, hoping to throw off the stalker and nearly ran over a tall, dark-skinned woman coming her way.

Petra stammered an apology before realizing who she was speaking to, and relief flooded over her. She felt a genuine smile form on her lips. This was Chantal Stone, one of the Koupe Tribinal, the court that meted out justice in the city.

The court that took a very dim view of criminals stalking people on the street.

She heard the steps behind her, but she was no longer afraid. Meeting Chantal Stone on the street was like finding out the Terminator was sent to protect you.

A man came around the corner at a jog, saw the two women standing there and started backpedaling. He fell over in his attempt to reverse the direction of his charge, landing on his ass and crab walking backward. The tall woman raised her eyebrows.

"I was just... I need to tell her something." He nodded at Petra.

"Then tell us all," Chantal said.

Petra was surprised at the speed and efficacy of the men who appeared from the shadows and grabbed the man who'd been following her. He was beaten into submission, an act of overt violence that Petra couldn't watch before he was dragged away into the darkness of an alley. The rumor was that if you were hauled into the Cut Court, you never would return. Petra never wanted to find out if it was true.

"It's not wise to be out on the street on your own," Chantal said.

"I know. I was meeting friends, but they weren't where they said they'd be," Petra said, realizing what a lame excuse it was and dropping her gaze to the sidewalk.

"I will send you home with an escort, and don't let me find you out on these streets alone ever again. Do you understand?" Chantal's eyes were a piercing as Petra's father's.

Petra nodded, and when two more men appeared from the shadows, she went without demurring. She might be naive enough to defy her father, but she would not risk finding herself brought before the Koupe Tribinal for something as trivial as a party.

CHAPTER ELEVEN

Melvin dragged his battered bicycle up the steps from the basement. The steps were steep and narrow and the bike unwieldy. But the trip to his supply house was many miles long and necessitated a vehicle of some sort. He was thankful for it but wished he didn't need to hide it in such an inconvenient location. It added fifteen minutes to his trip on each end.

He settled his mostly empty backpack over his shoulders and pedaled down the center of the street and then headed south along the river. Dusk was falling, which was both good and bad. Good in that there were fewer people on the streets, and bad because those who remained tended to be scarier, and more likely to ambush him and drag him off his bike.

A little over two hours of biking down I-75 and he was in Rockwood, riding along Heron River Drive toward the Michigan River. It was nearing full dark now, but he knew his way by heart and the moon reached the road, giving him just enough light to see the driveway of an abandoned marine supply and repair shop. He rode around back of the warehouse-sized building, leaned his bike against the wall and knocked on the glass door.

The curtain twitched, an eye peered out, and the locks began turning. The door opened to a slight man who ushered him in and quickly closed and locked the door. Melvin waited for him to secure the door and then the two men shook hands warmly.

"Roger," Melvin said. "How have you been? Have there been any more raids?"

"They came again a week ago," Roger said, leading the way through the office and into the room that used to contain the bits and pieces used to repair boats of all sizes. It was lined with shelves holding boxes of every size, many with a red cross or the twined snake symbol of the medical profession. "We took a hit on the usual supplies, sterile bandages, wraps, and chuck pads. But they still haven't discovered the vault. And I don't mean them to ever find it."

He was talking about the basement storage rooms where they stored the more valuable items. Pieces of equipment, antibiotics, sterile saline, and uncontaminated water were among the supplies they kept there. Raids were inevitable, they'd long since stopped moving from place to place in an effort to outwit the Tribuinal, but if all they ever found were boxes of bandages and sterile dressings, then Melvin could live with that.

"Do we have soup packets?" he asked. "I'm almost out."

"Let's go down and get you loaded up." Roger led the way to a door that opened into a broom closet where he pushed on the back wall, causing the wall next to him to slide back, revealing the stairway to the basement. Roger and Melvin were the only people on this Earth who knew about the secret panel, and they meant to keep it that way. When they'd discovered the place the door had opened onto the top landing of the staircase, and it had been a simple thing to enclose it and disguise the entrance as a broom closet.

The secrecy meant they had to haul all the deliveries to the basement themselves, a sometimes lengthy and back-breaking job. Especially since the two men didn't let the delivery drivers into the building at all but made them drop their boxes on the loading dock and leave before they took them inside.

At the bottom of the stairs, they turned down a long hall and through a doorway into what used to be a drydock for boat repair. The lower half of the boat would rest down here, giving workmen access to the propeller and hull, while the deck was accessible from above. But the opening had been closed over when the shop had transformed from mostly repairs to mostly sales. And this suited Melvin and Roger just fine.

Melvin moved deftly among the shelves that filled the room, picking and choosing the supplies he would take back to the city. Antibiotics in many forms -- pills, injectable, and ointment -- dressings, adhesive bandages, ticking them off his mental list as he walked along the rows of shelves. Next to a pallet stacked with boxes of dried soup Melvin pulled a couple of grocery bags from a pocket of his backpack and filled them with soup packets. He tossed the discarded cartons into a trash bin.

It was while he was trying to decide if he should bring more than one roll of fiberglass cast that the banging started. He shot a startled look at Roger.

"Stay here," Roger said. "I'm going to lock you in."

"My bike..." Melvin began, but Roger cut him off.

"I'll deal with it," he said and closed the door, locking Melvin in.

Melvin knew he could get out if he really needed to do so.

There were actually two exits, one through the door they'd come in through, and the other a garbage chute where the detritus of boat repair used to be dumped. It spilled out into a ditch beneath the building, and if need be, he could crawl out from underneath on his hands and knees. He supposed it still was oily and gross, but if he had to, he could do it.

"I don't know why you've bothered to come back," Roger was saying from above. The floor didn't muffle the conversation much at all. "You raided me a few nights ago, and we haven't had a shipment, I've nothing more to give you."

"Whose bike is this?" an angry voice asked. "Doesn't it belong to Melvin Foles?"

"Yeah, but he's not here. He had a flat last time he was down here, ran over a screw in the yard. I fixed it for him. He'll have to walk down here to get it, or catch a ride somehow," Roger said. "Or just steal another bicycle, I suppose."

Melvin could tell Roger was nervous, there was an almost imperceptible tremor in his voice that Melvin hoped the Cut Court's thug couldn't hear. But that was unrealistic. The court only hired men whose instincts were finely tuned. And while Roger could be nervous about any number of things, including there being a gun trained on him, Melvin couldn't wait to see how this turned out. If it went badly, he needed to be long gone.

"I want to search," the thug was saying.

Melvin already was turning away when he heard Roger consent to the search. He needed to be out of here, just in case. He walked swiftly and silently to that hatch in the floor. It was located in the center of the main drydock, the cement slab sloping toward it.

He unlatched the grate that covered the chute and lifted it. The aperture was just large enough for him to slide through on the diagonal. He gathered his supplies, dumping two backpacks and two grocery bags through the hole. Then he latched his fingers through the inside of the grate, jammed his feet against opposite sides of the metal duct, and attempted to close the grill silently.

He wasn't successful, of course, but the ensuing thud was quieter than he had anticipated. He released his grip on both the grate and the metal tube and slid about fifteen feet, landing on his supplies. There wasn't much that could be broken, but the things that could were critical and he hoped he'd packed them well enough to survive the impact. He buckled the backpacks together and tied the grocery bags to one of the ties, then he slid one of the shoulder straps through the belt that held up his jeans and began crawling.

The space between the bottom of the ditch and the floor of the building above him wasn't quite tall enough for him to crawl on his hands and knees. He tried a kind of crouching crawl, but it was uncomfortable and not very efficient, so he switched to dragging himself along by his elbows while pushing himself forward with his toes. It was faster than it sounds and a few minutes later he emerged out from under the back side of the building and slid down a small hill, catching himself at the edge of the stream.

He didn't dare check to see if his bicycle was being guarded, although he dreaded the long march home. He carried his bags across the stream and up the other side of the bank, coming out on the road he'd ridden in on. Melvin looked at his watch, an old Timex wind-up he'd found in an abandoned apartment, and gave himself five minutes on the road. After that, he'd make his way through the brush of the greenbelt, and the backyards of the houses lining the street near the town.

He'd been walking for three minutes when he heard the gunshots. He hoped fervently that Roger had not been killed.

He wanted to go back to check on him, but that would be foolish. Melvin stood resolute in the middle of the road for another thirty seconds before he heard a vehicle. He threw himself into the brush and lay with the odor of decaying leaves under his nose until the car had passed.

He swore under his breath, stashed his bags where he could find them again and ran down the road back to the warehouse. He barely noticed his bicycle lying mangled in the parking lot as he made his way to the door. It had been left open. He called Roger's name and heard a sound at the far end of the big room.

He found Roger near the secret entrance to their warehouse, blood oozing from his chest. He was appalled and angry that they would kill this man because they couldn't find the one they really wanted. He wanted to scream, but he kept his voice light.

"Had to be the hero, did you?" he said, rolling his jacket and placing it under Roger's head.

Roger smiled wanly. "You know me, never learned to keep my mouth shut when a good put-down comes to mind. Am I dead?"

"I'm afraid so. To tell you the truth I'm surprised you're still talking. You always were a stubborn bastard." Melvin pulled off his long sleeve shirt and then his T-shirt, wadding it up and pressing it into the wound.

"Don't bother with that," Roger said, "it's a waste of resources." He huffed out a weak laugh.

"The world is not short of T-shirts," Melvin countered. "Shut up. No, I take that back, don't shut up. Tell me what I need to know to keep this going." He glanced around the building.

"First, move. You need a new location," Roger wheezed. "Second, find out what fool is ratting us out to the Court and shoot him. Get your own van so you can't be ratted out. Or a boat, just some way to move stuff, so you aren't reliant on assholes. And put a hole in the bastard who killed me." He gave Melvin a tremulous smile. "I thought I might live a little longer than this."

"Don't worry," Melvin said, doing his best to keep his sorrow and rage from his voice and face. He did so want Roger's passing to be peaceful. "I'll kill the murdering bastards and the murdering bastards' boss. You will be avenged."

Roger nodded. A look of satisfaction crossed his face, and the smile appeared again. Then his eyes closed for the last time and he stopped breathing. Melvin sat with Roger a few minutes more. He had vague ideas of it taking a few minutes for the spirit to pass. Only when he thought he saw a shift in Rogers body, a kind of deflation, did he get up.

He walked to the other end of the building and screamed "Fuck!" as loudly as he could, over and over, until his voice wore out. Then he went in search of a shovel.

He dug the grave in the softer soil on the other side of the stream. He wasn't used to shoveling, and it wasn't long before his back and shoulders were aching. The constant burn in his biceps helped to keep his mind off his rage and on the sanctity of the burial. He was not a barbarian.

If he had been, he would have tossed Roger's body into the river and let it go where it may. Dawn was breaking when he carried Roger's body across the stream and laid him in the grave. When Roger was arranged with as much dignity as an Egyptian Pharaoh, with small flat stones over his eyes, Melvin climbed out of the grave. He said a short prayer in the early morning chill and began shoveling dirt back into the grave. It was mid-morning when he finished.

He walked up the street in full sunlight knowing that if he didn't clear out the medical supplies soon, someone would find them and clean him out. Roger had been the deterrent, his watchman, and he could act like a crazy-man so convincingly that people liked to try their luck elsewhere after dealing with his banshee yells. Roger would be missed in so many ways. Where would he find another person he could trust?

CHAPTER TWELVE

MELVIN WAS NOT in the apartment when Glen arose the next morning, and he didn't know if he should be worried. Maybe Melvin didn't come home every morning. He'd said he was going for supplies, maybe it took longer than a night to get there and back again. Not knowing if he should worry, he decided not to do so. One way or the other, he eventually would know, and until then worrying was a waste of energy.

He busied himself in the kitchen, making breakfast out of the oatmeal, some dried apples, and a cinnamon stick he found in the back of the cupboard. He found some instant coffee and heated water for that as well. The range was fueled by propane, and while the supply to the building long had been exhausted, there was a small, outdoor grill-sized tank hooked up. The oven controls were electronic, and Glen didn't know how to bypass that hurdle but, if push came to shove, if they wanted to bake something, they could do that on the range top too.

The oatmeal just was starting to smell good when Mia came shuffling out of the hallway, running her hands through her hair. Her eyes were swollen, puffy really, and he thought she had been crying. Well, who could blame her? He'd cry too if he came home to find everyone gone, but all their possessions still right where they'd left them. It had to be a terrible shock.

"Where's Melvin?" she asked, looking around. "Hasn't he gotten back yet?"

"I haven't seen him," Glen said. "But he could have come back and gone out again. I don't know what his life pattern is like."

"Should we be worried?" she asked, lifting the lid and sniffing the oatmeal in the pot.

"I wouldn't bother worrying. We'll wait, see what turns up, and then deal with that reality. There really is no point in worrying." And he believed that, but he couldn't shut down the nagging feeling in the back of his mind that he should be doing something.

Initially, Glen's plans for the day were to go back to the library and treat the sick and injured, and when Christian and Sally shuffled in, sniffing the air, he said as much. "As soon as you all are ready to go, we'll go," he added.

"So, we're going to treat people on the steps of the library?" Sally asked. "How long do you think until someone runs us off?"

"She has a point," Christian said through a mouthful of oats. "Eventually, someone will take offense. They always do. A petty bureaucrat will come along and ask for our permit, confiscate everything, and fine us. We should avoid that if we can."

"Don't talk with your mouth full," Mia reproached him. She looked around. "Could we run a clinic out of here, do you think?"

"No," Glen said. "I don't like this as the location. The other people in the building might object, and there'd be people in the back courtyard day and night. We need an abandoned building. I'll ask Melvin about that when he gets back."

"What?" Sally looked up in alarm, "Melvin's not back?"

"We aren't worrying," Mia told her. "Who knows what kind of schedule he keeps."

Sally nodded but didn't look happy. She tapped her spoon on the polished dark wood table and bit her lip.

"With the right facility," Mia said, "we could set up a small surgery room. Although, sterilization might be an issue. Is there a shortage of bleach, do you think?"

"Anesthetic, or rather the lack of it, would be the greater deterrent," Glen said. "Unless you propose we knock them over the head whenever they seem to be regaining consciousness."

"People would flock to us," Christian said drily. "Come have your broken bones set, and get a concussion for free. I think we might have more of an issue with those doctors in the upper floors of the hospital. If we start treating people for free – or at least at rates that normal people can afford – they might take exception."

"I don't know why," Sally said. "It's not like we'd be poaching any of their patients."

"No, but their patients might start protesting at being charged so much when poor people are getting treated for free," Glen said. He also thought it likely that whoever was in charge of the doctors wouldn't like their monopoly to be challenged. There would be plenty of challenges, not the least of which would be the number of people with conditions that had gone untreated for a very long time.

"Maybe there's an abandoned medical clinic we could set up in," Mia said. "We could scavenge equipment from the lower floors of the hospitals. If there is anything left to be scavenged. Do you think everything, everywhere is already long gone?" She looked worried.

"Don't know," Christian said, "but I bet Melvin knows. You could ask him, or go look for yourself. We might fare better in a dental office. I think people avoid dental offices, but they'd have pretty good equipment. And are probably pretty easy to sterilize."

"I'm almost convinced it would be easier to set up in an empty room. It would be easier to sterilize than a room with a bunch of equipment to work around." Glen said. "But wherever it is, it should be close to the community that it serves. Preferably, right in the middle of it."

"Maybe there are rooms in the basement of the library?" Sally said. "That would be convenient."

"Let's not inhabit a basement," Mia said. "Surely some rooms let in lots of nice natural light. Working by glow sick and candlelight is not my idea of a good time."

"Nor mine," Glen said. "I agree with lots of natural light. Although in this city it seems to be dark everywhere, all the time."

"Maybe at the top of one of the tall buildings?" Christian, and then answered himself. "No, because people would have to walk up all those flights of stairs. Maybe we'll have to use mirrors to increase the light."

"Or find a generator and a source of fuel," Mia said.

"A waterwheel could generate electricity," Sally said. "Somewhere on the river?"

"Let's wait and ask Melvin what he thinks," Glen said, secretly hoping the man hadn't met with misadventure.

Not long after their breakfast conversation, they left the apartment for the shallow library steps, skirting through the back alley and out onto the street. They expected at least a few people to be waiting for them in the courtyard in front of the library, at the very least those whom they had treated and told to come back. But when they reached the library, the line of waiting patients snaked around the stalls in the market, down the block, and around the corner.

"At least we won't feel un-needed," Sally said.

"Or bored," Christian added.

"Or like we can take even a moment for ourselves to go pee," Mia groaned.

But Glen felt something akin to happiness and smiled. "Let's get to work," he said.

It took Melvin seven hours to walk back to the city. He carried one backpack on his back and the other on his front, the bags of soup bumping against his thighs. It was frustrating to have to travel so slowly, but not only did he have the weight of the backpacks he also had to stay out of sight. A single man carrying a load of gear was a target. Once, in the past, he'd been set upon by a group of preteens. They'd ripped his bundles away from him, and it was only the appearance of one of their parents that kept him from being beaten to death. Now he merely remained unseen.

Only it wasn't that simple. The most direct route was back along the freeway. The benefits of that were you could see people coming, but that also meant they could see you. He scanned for high places where lookouts could be waiting, trying to determine early if he needed to get undercover.

For a while, he walked in the ditch between the north and south lanes. He couldn't be seen by the casual observer, but if there was a lookout on an overpass, it was likely he would be trapped with no viable means of escape. So, he did his best to dart from vehicle to vehicle, hiding behind stranded cars and trucks. The buses were the best because they sat low, but their windows were high, and he could walk beside them without crouching and also without fear of being seen. It was tiring, this constant need to scout for an escape route or place to hide. His back and thighs ached from stooping over as he tried to remain hidden behind the vehicles.

When he reached the outskirts of the city, he began looking for another bicycle. He didn't like the odds that he would make it home carrying these goods on foot. But it wasn't easy to find transportation, a bicycle lock being a simple mechanism unaffected by the EMP, which you couldn't break without specialized tools.

He did eventually spot an abandoned bike in a junk pile. It was far too small for him and had a 1970s banana seat, ridiculous and uncomfortable, but it was faster than walking and would give him a little maneuverability. One of the tires was mostly flat, but he shrugged and rode it anyway. What did it matter if he ruined the rim? It's only job was keeping him alive this one night.

In the back of his mind Melvin knew the bike might not make it all the way back to his neighborhood. So, he kept his eyes open for a replacement, while also scanning to make sure he wasn't trapped by a gang of marauders. About five blocks later the tire came off the rim. He tried to keep riding but the tireless wheel didn't handle well, making it practically impossible to steer and he had to abandon it.

It wasn't long after that that his fears materialized. As he walked down the center of the street, two young men stepped into his line of sight. They were half a block in front of him, and when he glanced behind there were two more young men not far behind. He glanced frantically up and down the street, looking for an escape. An open building, an alleyway, somewhere they would have to run single file. If he could get there first, there might be a chance.

All the while he was looking, more and more black-clad gang members joined the others in front of and behind him. He thought he saw a break between buildings on his right, so he started moving left in what he hoped was a diversionary tactic. He was just about to make a mad dash across the street and into the alley when he heard a sound to his left.

A quick glance showed him a metal gate with a woman standing behind it, and he hesitated.

"Come in here," she said. "Quickly, or they'll catch you."

He only had a moment to make up his mind, and he knew it could be a trap, but again it was a narrow space, and he'd just have to get past one person before he legged it out of there.

"Come on!" she hissed, and he abruptly turned and sprinted toward her location.

There was a shout behind him, and the gang of thugs suddenly was running. They were shouting at each other to not let him get away. But he reached the gate, and the woman let him in, slamming it shut, throwing bolts and securing them with padlocks. Then she turned and ran, instructing him to follow.

They ran along the narrow gap between the buildings, his backpacks catching on the rough brick exteriors. The woman led him down a steep set of stairs to a door, which she unlocked using the key she had hanging around her neck. He followed her into a wet basement with little light and hoped like hell this wasn't a mistake.

"This way," she said again, and led him through winding passages until he was so turned around he thought he might be lost there forever if she abandoned him. But she did not. Eventually, they came up to a set of stairs, and they climbed out of the basement onto the first-floor landing. There she turned and faced him, a knife clutched in her hand.

"You didn't bring me all this way just to kill me, did you?" he asked. Of course, that would have been an excellent way to wear him down if she thought she would have to fight him, but if that was the case why rescue him at all?

"I want one of your backpacks," she said. "You go free, with half your loot, but I get the other half for saving you."

Melvin felt his face fall. He'd carried these backpacks for

more than sixteen miles, only to have one of them taken from him. Disappointment flooded through him. He should've made a dash for the other side of the street.

"And what if I refuse?" he asked. "I could overpower you."

"If you refuse, I scream, and then my brothers, who wait for me upstairs," she nodded upward, "will come and kill you. Then I will have all, and you will have nothing. Not even your life."

He wondered if she was bluffing. Was there really anyone waiting up the stairs? He didn't know. "There are many things in my bags that you need specialized knowledge to use," he said. "What if I give you one bag of soup?" He pointed to one of the grocery bags dangling at his side before continuing, "and gauze bandages, antibiotic cream, medical tape, and painkillers? Would that do?"

"What else do you have?" she asked, brushing the dark bangs from her eyes with her fingers.

"Fiberglass casts," he said. "But you have to know how to use them, or they're useless. Some bottles of injectable antibiotics and syringes, but again you have to know the doses and how to use them or you could make things worse."

"What else can you give me?" she asked.

An idea came to him and he suddenly had some hope for his supplies.

"I know a doctor," he said, "and if you let me pass, he will treat you for the rest of your life for free."

"And how do you know he will treat me?" she asked.

"Because I supply him with his medical supplies. If I ask him to treat you, he will." Melvin looked at her intently.

"And my children?" she asked.

"Your children, your brothers and sisters, your mother and father, your half-brother once removed for all I care. Let me pass, and we will treat you. For free."

"And I can have the soup and the bandages?" She looked

at him hopefully, while also making little stabbing motions with her knife.

Melvin dropped both backpacks onto the ground. He untied one of the bags of soup and handed it to her, then he opened the packs, took a quarter of the sterile bandages, some tubes of ointment and some rolls of medical tape and dumped them in the bags with the soup.

"I want you to write it down for me," she said, watching him intently.

"What do you want me to write?" he asked.

"That you promise to treat my family for free for the rest of your life." She paused for a minute, thinking. "And that your heirs will treat my heirs inpet-, imper-, oh, forever."

"Do you have a pen?" he asked.

"You don't have a pen in that bag? You must have everything else." She searched around her person for a while. "You'll have to write it in blood then."

"I may have something," he said grimly and rummaged in a pocket of his backpack until a pencil came to hand. "Give me one of those packages," he said.

She gave him one of the gauze packages, and he wrote on the paper backing. 'I, Melvin Foles, agree to treat...' he looked up. "What's your name?"

"Just put, 'The bearer of this note,'" she said.

He nodded although he thought it was hard luck on him. He'd be taking care of her and all her friends, and then someone would steal it, and then he'd have to treat that group, and probably they'd start making money by renting the note out to other people. '...the bearer of this note, who as of this date, is a female of approximately thirty years old, with brown eyes and hair, about five feet five inches tall. I also agree to treat her progeny, siblings, parents and other FAMILY members so long as I, or my progeny, are practicing medicine.' Then he signed and dated it.

Her eyes were shining, and she held out her hand, but he pulled the note and her bag of supplies close to his body. "You promise there is no one out there waiting to jump me?" He asked.

She nodded.

"You will not try and stab me as I go through the door?"

Again she nodded.

"Wait," she said, "how do I find you?"

"My name is on this," he indicated the package he'd written on, "I'm Melvin Foles. Ask around for the man who gives out soup. You'll find me soon enough. Now, is there anything that you are not telling me that could end up hurting me?"

This time she shook her head.

Melvin shrugged inwardly and handed her the bag. She grabbed it from him, and for a moment he thought she would bolt, but she turned, unlocked the door and let him leave. Once through, she slammed the door, and he heard it lock behind him. He stood for a moment listening, hoping like hell this wasn't a trap. But no sounds were forthcoming, and when he went to walk through the foyer out to the street, no one stopped him.

It took Melvin a few minutes to figure out where he was. He had walked every street in the city, but mostly at night and not much in this area. But he eventually found a couple of street signs that hadn't been torn down and was able to reorient himself. Two hours later he was back home again.

CHAPTER THIRTEEN

Chantal Stone stood at the tall windows of her top floor condo and surveyed the city. It was calm in the early morning, quiet. She loved the peace of it, while the worst of the city still slept. The worst of the criminals were creatures of the darkness, even now when daylight only brought shadows to the streets.

Up here, above much of the city, there was light. The sun streamed into her home, a bright and welcoming place that had been hers since long before the event that had changed everything. She had defended this place, her home, and she would not relinquish it. The long climb up the stairs at the end of the day strengthened her, kept her stamina from deserting her.

Unlike the street dwellers, Chantal could see what this city could be. She knew what the town had been and what it would be again if given a chance. It would need to be tamed, yes, she knew that too. She smiled as she thought of it because she would be the one to tame it.

As she turned from the view, the sunlight reflected off the

revolver as she holstered it on her hip. A rainbow of light flickered across the ceiling as she left the room.

As she descended the stairs, she thought about her latest problem, Melvin Foles. If he could not be controlled, he would have to be eliminated. The power of the Koupe Tribinal would not be questioned. Could not be questioned. If they were not feared, they could not rule. The memory of Melvin Foles's demise would live in this city's DNA for years to come. The Koupe would rule.

As she exited the building, she was approached by one of her enforcers. He went down on one knee in front of her on the sidewalk, as was proper, and then stood, head bowed.

"What is it, enforcer?" she said. She had adopted this way of speaking to her employees. She wanted to impersonalize them, so they saw her as someone to be respected and never disobeyed. A mere employer did not garner that level of respect and obedience.

"We were not able to apprehend Melvin Foles," he said, his gaze still on the sidewalk.

"No?" She spoke only the one syllable but filled it with menace.

"We killed his accomplice at the warehouse." His gaze flicked to her face for just a moment before returning to the sidewalk. He was looking for praise.

"You've killed his partner, then?" She didn't let the rage that filled her show on her face, even though she would have liked to strike him. "And what do you think will happen now?"

The man looked puzzled. "In what way, Judge Stone?"

"Do you think that Melvin will continue using that building to house his supplies?" Her voice was deadly calm, which pleased her. She wanted to throttle him.

"I wouldn't," he said, puzzled.

"So how do you propose we find his supply house, now?" she asked.

"Follow him?" he said, his voice hushed.

"And if he's afraid for his life, do you think he will be easy to follow?"

He hung his head.

"And what did Foles' partner do that he deserved to die?" she asked.

"He was lying." The eyes came up now. He was sure about this. "He wouldn't tell us where Melvin Foles was, and I could tell by his eyes he knew."

"And he deserved to die for that?" She hoped he would catch on soon, or she would kill him here and be done with it.

He remained quiet, not knowing the answer, she thought. She shook her head at the idiocy.

"Who makes life and death decisions?" she asked.

"The Koupe Tribinal," he said.

"And are you a member of the Court?" She was so impatient with this game her palms where itching, But she maintained her air of patience.

"No."

"What happens to people who don't abide by the rules set down by the Court?"

His face blanched and he looked at her pleadingly, licking his lips nervously.

"Come with me," she said and turned to walk to the Court's rooms.

The man turned and followed her obediently.

They walked through the streets lined with people living in vehicles. Mostly the streets were deserted, but here and there were signs of morning life. In a patch of green with a swing set a man had his hand raised, about to strike a child. But he lowered it when he saw Chantal. Judge Stone was a familiar sight on these streets, and everyone knew what happened when she caught you doing something she didn't agree with.

She stood utterly still, her eyes steady upon the man. He began backing away from the child. The girl, seeing her opening, slid off the swing and ran across the park. Chantal hoped she was headed home to her mother, and not running away. But one couldn't know these things, and they moved on, leaving the man frozen in place, looking after them.

A little further on, a tired-looking mother was trying to wrangle a child into a coat. Chantal thought the boy was maybe five or six years old. She knelt down next to him and waited until he looked her in the eyes before she spoke.

"Do you know about Judge Stone?" She knew that parents used her as the local boogeyman, and she used that to her advantage.

The child nodded.

"I am Judge Stone."

The child's lower lip began quivering, and the mother snatched the child away and pulled on his jacket. She pressed the child behind her and thanked Chantal in quavering words. Chantal touched the woman on her shoulder and turned away. She felt that if she turned to look, she'd see the woman brushing that shoulder with her hand. Sweeping the evil away. The thought made her smile.

The next two groups of people she passed drew away from her as she approached. One of the families stepped out into the street, around the other side of their old Toyota SUV-turned-home. The feeling she got when people shrank from her delighted her. She had power. She held their lives in her hands, and they knew it. Ruling by fear was underrated. If the powerful knew how much satisfaction could be derived from unquestioning obedience, they all would use it.

Before long they turned down the dark alley, yes, dark even in the morning, and down the stone steps and under the sign of the jackal, torches burning on either side. As they entered the hallway, she turned to her enforcer. "Stay here." She moved farther into the chamber and slid through the tiny hall to the room where the judges congregated and made their decisions.

Arthur and Xander already were there, sitting at the end of the long table, laughing about something. The three of them -- Arthur, Xander, and Chantal -- were the main pillars of the court. There were others, of course, sometimes so many that the long table wouldn't hold them all. But they were the three key players.

"Gentlemen," she nodded her head at them as she pulled out a chair. "I have a problem."

They gave her their undivided attention as she explained the action her enforcers had taken at Melvin Foles' supply house, their expressions grave.

"He must be executed, of course," Xander said. "It's the punishment for acting against the best interests of the Tribinal. We cannot be seen to show favor for our own."

"But he clearly thought he was acting on our behalf," Arthur countered, his brown eyes boring into Xander's blue. "He did not do wrong on purpose, he made a mistake. If everyone who made a mistake were to be executed, there would be no one left and the last man standing would have to kill himself. Also a crime."

"His mistake, as you say," Xander countered, "was to kill a man. That is always punishable by death. That is written in our law. There are no exceptions."

"But we don't know if he killed the man in self-defense, or if it was accidental," Arthur replied. "Surely the circumstances are important. We should bring him before the Court."

"Agreed." Xander nodded solemnly.

"Yes," Chantal said. "Three or five judges? I think three."

"Agreed." Xander and Arthur nodded.

"I'll find an enforcer to herald him in," Arthur said, and left the room in the opposite direction from where Chantal had entered. He was back a few minutes later. "We can go in."

Xander grabbed his mask from its hook on the wall and slid it over the top half of his face, leaving his mouth and chin visible. Chantal hated that mask, it was pretentious and theatrical, a slap to the serious work they performed in the Tribinal. But he would not be swayed from wearing it, as he believed it struck fear into the hearts of those who had seen it.

And maybe it did strike fear into people, although Chantal privately thought the place itself did the job well enough. Too much fear and all they could do was blather. It was not good practice to convict criminals who could not speak for themselves. There had to be standards, or the people would turn. It was good to rule by fear, but there had to be rules. The populace had to know when they were doing wrong, or they would revolt. Their minds could not deal with the inconsistencies.

She heard her errant enforcer being called into the court chamber. She knew they would be pushing him to his knees, tying his hands behind his back. She felt sorry for him, in a way. He would think that his life was over now, and he wouldn't be sure why. He would know from having been in the room that it didn't always end in death and that death would be preferred over some of the punishments. And he wouldn't know what awaited him.

She entered the chamber with the other two judges and sat in the high-backed chair at the center of the dais. Arthur and Xander sat on either side. The other chairs had been removed from the stage, and the three remaining were lit by tall pillar candles so that the three judges' faces were illuminated but little else.

"Enforcer," boomed Xander, "do you know your crime?"

"It wasn't just me, Judge Marcus, there were two men with me," the enforcer said. He looked small in the circle of dim light, not at all like the large and muscular man that he was.

Chantal could smell his fear, see his natural courage shrink away. That is what the Court did to you. What it was created to do. And even when you'd seen the devices of fear in action, when it came to be your turn, you too were afraid.

"Do you know your crime?" Xander repeated.

"I killed a man," the enforcer said.

Chantal could hear the despair. She thought he was regretting having told her what they'd done. She wondered where the other men had gone. Far from Detroit, she thought. As far as they could get from their inevitable death. It would be waiting here if they ever returned.

"Indeed." It was Arthur's turn now. "And what is the punishment for killing the innocent?"

"But he wasn't innocent," the enforcer protested. "He was helping Melvin Foles. He was aiding and abetting."

"Was he the man we asked you to bring to us?" Arthur asked.

The enforcer didn't speak, just looked at the dirt under his knees.

"Is it your responsibility to decide who dies and who lives?" Chantal asked.

The enforcer shook his head mutely.

"Does anyone die without first coming here to be tried?" Xander asked.

The enforcer's head dropped even closer to the ground.

"The consequence of murder is death," Chantal chanted. "Are we agreed?"

"No," Arthur said. "This man was doing our bidding to the best of his ability. I do not believe he should die for that."

Chantal turned to Xander, "Do you agree?" she asked.

"No." Xander shook his masked head, making the shadows dance around them. "The punishment remains the same regardless of the circumstances."

"What punishment do you condone?" she asked Arthur.

"Take his right hand as a reminder of what is right and just," Arthur said.

"Very well, I will decide," Chantal said, and she rose and left the dais. Arthur and Xander followed suit, and the three slid through the hidden passageway.

Chantal asked to be left alone in the debating room, and both Xander and Arthur slipped away. She sat at the large table and looked at her reflection in its polished surface. This was the problematic part, balancing the punishment against the crime, and the effect of the crime on the populace.

She didn't want to appear emotional. All decisions must seem to be logical, and the crime must fit the punishment. So, here she had a man who'd taken the law into his own hands, who had murdered a man because he was associated with the man he was tracking. He had acted far beyond his authority, overstepping all bounds. The power of the position turned his head, and he had taken on the role of judge, jury and executioner.

But he had done so at the Court's behest. He had believed himself to be doing the right thing. But didn't criminals always think they were doing the right thing? No. No, sometimes they knew they were doing the wrong thing, and they did it anyway. That was not the enforcer's crime. This crime was to do his job with too much zeal.

And what would happen if she killed this man? Would she have trouble finding new enforcers? Or would there still be plenty who would be willing to do her bidding for the reward of suitable housing and plentiful food? And power, there was always that as well. And the protection of the Court.

Although, what good was the protection of the Court if you were executed for performing your duties?

This last point convinced her. Stood and made her way back through the passage into the Court.

Her enforcer still was kneeling, his head bowed so low she thought his forehead must be resting on the dirt. He had been a decent enforcer, if not strictly obedient. He used his initiative. Many enforcers had no ambition. A deep sadness fell over her, the judge's mantle like a weight weighing her down. She took a deep breath.

"Enforcer," she proclaimed, "you have served the Koupe Tribinal well, and we are grateful for your service. However, you have made a grave mistake, and for this, you will lose your right hand as well as your position as an enforcer for this Court. Have you anything to say?"

He lifted his head slowly. "Judge Stone," he said, "I would beg that you take my life. There is no existence, no real life in this place, for a man with only one hand. I would die a slow and horrible death or be kicked to death in the street. Take my life now and spare me that fate."

"This is what you truly want?" Chantel asked.

He looked her directly in the eyes. "Yes, judge, this is what I want. It is the fate I prefer."

"So be it." She stood, nodded to her executioner, and left the room. Ordinarily, she might have stayed to witness the honor of his death, but she could not, for she could not risk her people seeing her weakness.

She retired to her office, her sanctuary, where no one would disturb her, and wept for the first time in many years. Why this one man should affect her, she did not know. Perhaps it was that he had pleaded for death instead of life. He was the first to do so since she had created the Tribinal. Many had begged for their lives, would have accepted the loss of a hand as mercy. But not this man, this enforcer. She felt honored to have worked with him, and she did not even know his name.

Later, when she had come to terms with her emotions, she made her way back to the judge's chamber and sat at the table with Arthur and Xander. When they questioned her with their eyes, she waved their concern away. "Let us speak of Melvin Foles," she said. "I think we should take him from his home."

"Are you sure, Chantal?" Arthur asked. "We have yet to invade the sanctity of the home. We named the home inviolate. Are you sure you wish to change this over one man?"

"I do," she said. "A good man died today because of Melvin Foles, and I'm tired of chasing him. We will go to his home, and we will bring him here."

"Wait," Arthur said. "You sentenced the enforcer to death?"

"No," she said, "I sentenced him to maiming, and he begged for death. I granted his wish. That's all."

"Smart man," Xander said, smiling.

Arthur looked pained. "He asked for death rather than live with one hand," he said under his breath, shaking his head. "That was an unnecessary loss of life." His mouth pulled down at the corners.

Chantel got up and walked to the door. "Send in our largest enforcer," she called. And returned to her chair.

A moment later a large man walked into the room. He was by far the most massive man she ever had seen, although he once had told her his brother was even larger. He stood well over six feet tall and was not one of those willowy basketball player types, but instead was built like a wrestler or a bodybuilder writ large. The offspring of a giant and a mortal. The thought made her smile, and she wondered when she began getting fanciful.

"We have a job for you, enforcer, and it's somewhat unusual," she said. "Can you obey without question?"

"Yes, judge," he said. "What is it that I can do for you?"

She pushed a folded piece of paper across the table. "Go to this address," she said, "and bring the man who lives there back alive. Do you understand? I want him alive."

"Of course Judge Stone," he replied, with military precision. "Go to his home, bring him here alive. Am I allowed to enter his home?"

"Yes. This one time, and this one time only, you may enter a home. But be sure you bring him here unharmed."

"Yes, judge," he said, and rose to go.

"One more thing," Xander said. "If there is anyone with him, they too must remain unharmed."

"Yes, judge," the enforcer said and left the room.

"Where have we gotten to?" Arthur asked. "We've reached the day where we have to remind our enforcers not to harm the innocent. That does not make me happy."

"But it was bound to happen," Chantel said. "Power corrupts the mind." And oh how she knew that to be true.

CHAPTER FOURTEEN

MIA KEPT her worrying about Melvin to herself. Glenn saw no reason to be concerned, and she didn't want to alarm the others, but her instincts told her he should've been back by now. She fretted as she led them out the back of the building, through a break in the chain link fence and down the alleyway out onto the street.

Glen's face lit up when he saw the number of people waiting to be treated at the library steps. The line wound around the block. Mia just felt tired. This would be another grueling day among a lifetime of grueling days. She knew she should not feel sorry for herself, she was alive and well and in good company, but she longed for laughter and fun. This business of struggling to stay alive day after day was not her idea of living.

She helped Glen and Sally set up a temporary med station, laying out supplies on a clean linen cloth that Glen had pilfered from the apartment. Then she went to stand at the head of the line. Sally assisted Glen, Christian kept peace among the waiting people, and Mia said, "Next patient, please," over and over again. After a while, she abandoned her post and went to stand in the shade under the elevated railway. She remembered it being called the people mover and wondered what it was called now. Obsolete, maybe, but that didn't seem like the appropriate word for something more advanced.

After what seemed forever, she caught Christian's eye and beckoned him over. "Let's go scouting for our new clinic," she said. "These people can police themselves. We're not really needed, and I feel like I'm wasting my time."

"Yeah," Christian said, "sure. I'm in."

They told Glen and Sally where they were going and headed out. They decided on a ten-by-five block grid and meant to walk to the northwesterly most corner and start from there. Only they eventually realize the street they were on was on the diagonal, cutting through their grid, and it wasn't clear where they were in relation to the northwestern point. So, they went back and started over, making sure they were walking on an east-west street.

It was quieter on this edge of their grid. It seemed people gathered together into communities, settling in areas where food and water were available. The river supplied both.

They walked east five blocks without seeing anything promising. The windows were busted out of many of the ground floor spaces, probably during the looting that happened after the space storm hit the Earth. Or perhaps the planet had hit the space storm? Who knew? Some scientist somewhere knew, but with no communication, they'd never be able to tell anyone. She spent a few minutes of their walk wondering what it might be like to be stranded at an observatory on top of a mountain. Lonely, she thought.

That first five blocks didn't yield anything that she or Christian thought was viable. For one thing, it seemed like too long a distance from the majority of the people. The second five blocks held an inordinate number of parking lots.

As they got closer to the center of town, they noticed more potential venues. One narrow but deep coffee shop still had its windows and doors, but on closer inspection seemed to be a bedroom for a host of men.

She and Christian moved on.

"They kind of reminded me of vampires," she said.

"Yeah," Christian replied, nodding his head, "me too. Very creepy."

They didn't bother looking at anything until they were well away from the area.

Before they knew it, they'd scoured the northern half of the grid and were passing the library again. As they walked by Glen and Sally, Glen raised his eyebrows at them. They shook their heads, and Glen frowned, apparently surprised that they had come this far without finding something suitable, but Mia wasn't surprised.

How many years had it been since the power had gone out? Three? Four? She was puzzled by her inability to figure that out. How many years had it been? She'd ask Glen later. The point was that it had been long enough for every inch of this city to be scoured. There was little left that still was usable but remained unclaimed. How were they to find what the thousands that lived in the town center had not?

They walked south of the library now, their mood somewhat dejected. By mid-afternoon, they'd walked the entire fifty-block grid and stood at the southwesterly most corner of their search area. Mia was tired, and her feet were sore. If she'd known she was going to be walking the entire city, she would have worn her hiking boots.

They were headed back toward the library, where Mia was hoping they'd be finishing up for the day. She hadn't slept well the previous night, and she'd love a nap. She spotted an empty bench in a small park and made a beeline for it, not even checking to see if Christian was following her. She just really needed to sit down. She ran across the road, not looking both ways – there was no need – and plunked herself on the bench, slipping off her shoes and wiggling her toes. When Christian sat beside her, she turned, using him to rest against, and put her feet up on the bench. It was heaven. Her socks breathed, and her feet felt the chill and liked it. It was almost like putting tired feet in a cold stream, she thought, letting the cold air revive them.

She opened her eyes and took in the view. Across from them, on the other side of the street from the park, was a squat stone building, maybe four stories high. It wasn't much to look at, bulky and square, too few windows that all were too small. But there, up near the roof, was a full balcony, and facing out onto that balcony – or maybe it was really a terrace – were a row of tall windows. Unbroken windows. She felt a spark of excitement.

"I bet those rooms get plenty of light," she said and pointed.

Christian followed her finger with his eyes, and a contemplative look crossed his face. He nudged her off his shoulder and got up. "Put your shoes on," he said. "I want to take a look."

So, she put the offending items back on her feet and followed him across the grass. They stood for a while on the sidewalk across from the building, looking up at the terrace and the windows beyond. There was no movement.

They crossed the street and looked at the three doors into the building. They were solid oak and carved elaborately. Mia went to the leftmost door and tried the handle. It wasn't just locked, it was tight and solid and moved about as much as a stone wall when she pulled on the handle. The other two doors were similarly impenetrable.

They walked around the building to the back, where they found the building was built in a U-shape around a courtyard. At the end of each wing were two more doors, similarly impenetrable but not nearly as imposing. The main body of the building, the bottom of the U, had French doors opening onto the courtyard. But they had been boarded up from the outside. However, over one of the doors at the end of the side wing was a small portico. Over the porch was a small window, which happened to be cracked open.

"Can you boost me up there?" she asked Christian.

He looked at the porch. "I don't know why not," he said and linked his hands.

She stepped into his hands, and he lifted her up until she could pull herself onto the roof. She used her hands and feet to work her way up to the ridgepole and then scooted to the wall where she very, very carefully stood up, using the wall as an anchor. The window was above her head, but she was able to reach the sill. She had a few nervous moments when she thought she was stuck, unable to go up and unable to go down, frozen against the wall until fatigue overtook her and she toppled to her death.

Well, okay, it wasn't that far down, so maybe not to her death. Still, it was bound to be painful, and potentially bone-breaking, so she'd better figure this thing out. She looked down at Christian, but he wasn't there. Her eyes sought and found him breaking a branch from a tree. As she watched he stripped the limb of twigs and a few dried up leaves and carried it over.

"Can you catch this?" he asked.

"Doubtful," she answered, afraid if she let go of the windowsill to grab for the branch her feet would slip, and she'd dangle one-handed until she fell. Likely impaling herself with the stick.

"Hold on then," Christian said and tossed the branch to the roof. Then he jumped, caught the gutter and swung his body up. He joined her on the ridgepole, standing close behind her, and used the stick to push up the sash.

"I'm going to sit on the ridgepole," he said in her ear, "and I want you to stand on my shoulders and see if you can pull yourself through the window. You should be small enough to make it. I couldn't get my shoulders through. Okay?"

"Sure," she said, "but with my luck I'll get in there, find myself in a locked closet and be stuck for life."

"Not for life," he said. "Just until I can convince you to crawl out again. I'm sitting now."

He slid down and balanced on the ridgepole. "Okay, now put your left foot on my shoulder and push yourself up."

She did as he said, steadying herself with her fingers on the windowsill. Of course, the problem was that when she was facing the wall, she couldn't get her foot up onto his shoulder. He slid his hand under her foot and lifted. As he pushed she levered her body through the window opening, pushed through and tumbled onto the floor.

She could have cried with relief. The time she climbed that massive tree in the forest to see where the town lay was nothing compared to balancing on the ridge of a roof with hardly anything to hold onto. She hadn't enjoyed it at all.

She opened her eyes and discovered she was in a bathroom. The door was open, and she could see down a hall. She got up and dusted herself off, leaning out the window to see Christian still sitting on the roof looking up.

"I'm in a bathroom," she said. "I'm going to take a look around."

"Go right ahead," he said, "but come back if you find anything interesting.

Out in the hall, she realized she was on a floor below the one she was interested in. Glancing in rooms as she walked down the hall in search of the stairwell she realized this building must be a museum. There were display cases, wall plaques, and photos on the walls that seemed to depict the history of the city. The rooms hadn't been looted, and she wondered why. Were the people of Detroit so respectful of its past that they wouldn't rob a museum?

She turned right, moving into the central wing of the building, and came upon the wide central stairs. They appeared to come up two flights to this floor, but no farther. However, a peek into the farther wing disclosed a narrower stairwell heading upward. She ran up the stairs two at a time and swung out onto the top floor. There was no hallway here, the stairs opening up into a large empty room with large arched windows lining the walls, and on one side, opening out onto the wide stone balcony.

Or at least they would open once the boards nailed across the width of the windows had been pried off. She didn't really know why this building had been left untouched, but she thought it might have something to do with how securely it had been made fast. Someone had cared a great deal about this place, so where were they now?

She took a good look at the space around her. It spanned the breadth and width of the central wing of the building. Empty but for the dust covering the floor and chandeliers. She went to peer out through a gap in the boards at the rear, but she could not see the end of the wing, where Christian was presumably still perched on the roof. She turned and ran back down the stairs, her heart pounding with anticipation. Wait until he saw this place.

When she reached the central staircase, she turned and ran down that too. When she reached the ground floor she went looking for the door under the porch roof. She padded down the hall, the floor of this wing seemingly was devoted to running the museum. There were offices, a dining room and finally a large kitchen before she discovered the short hallway off the kitchen that led to the back door.

It took a few minutes to figure out how to open the door. Not only did it have the regular deadbolt and handle lock, but also bolts that secured the door into the floor and upper frame as well, and that was on top of a metal bar fitted into slats on either side of the frame, preventing the door from being forced open. Someone really knew how to make a place secure.

But finally, she was through the door, which she propped open, and shouting at Christian to come down off the roof.

"Shut up, will you?" he hissed at her. "We don't want anyone else to know."

That indeed kept her quiet until he had joined her in the hall and they had relocked the door.

"You've got to see this place, Christian," she said, "It's wild."

They climbed the stairs, bypassing the ballroom, as Mia thought of it, and went all the way to the roof. This door, too, was barred. They opened it and stepped out onto a rooftop garden, the raised beds littered with dead vegetation that looked to have died in the frost. They walked the perimeter, looking down first onto the street, then the space between this building and its neighbor, the rear courtyard, and the driveway that gave street access to the rear of this building and the next.

"You'd have to be pretty determined to gain access via the roof. There's no easy way up or over," Christian said.

"It helps that the buildings on either side are lower and a good distance away. I don't think you could even jump from here to there," Mia pointed to the nearer building. "I couldn't do it, could you?"

"Doubtful," Christian said. "I wouldn't want to try it."

They relocked and barred the door, and Mia took him down to stare in awe at the ballroom.

"Plenty of natural light," he said, "but we'd have to haul a lot of furniture and equipment up here."

"We don't really need that much," she said. "After all, we're currently treating people on the shallow steps of the library. It would be nice if we had a desk and a bed. Then we could expand from there. I bet there's plenty of materials in this place to create a private examining room."

"Let's go see," Christian said.

Mia followed him from the room. The next floor down looked like it must have been a living museum. The rooms were decorated with furnishings from early Detroit — bedrooms, kitchen, a living room, servants' quarters, and a room full of leather harnesses and saddlery from the days before automobiles. The two floors below that were full of display cases, and art was mounted on the walls. One room was devoted to the stuffed carcasses of animals hunted during the early 1700s.

The floor below that was administrative offices, a large open foyer with a reception desk, and a private residence that took up the entire wing opposite from the side they entered through. The apartment puzzled Mia. It wasn't dust covered and felt lived in. The cupboards still had cans of food.

"It's like someone still lives here," Mia said.

"I know," Christian replied. "I feel like I'm trespassing."

They left the apartment and walked down the stairs into the basement. Here they found food storage, museum storage, rooms full of file cabinets, a shop piled with furniture that needed repairing, and partially finished display cases. Under the residence wing, they found a laundry, and past that a furnace room that housed not only a useless modern furnace but also an old-fashioned wood-burning octopus stove with heating ducts leading up into the building.

"I don't like that smell," Christian said, "but I think we need to see what it is." He pulled his shirt up over his nose.

They found the former resident of the apartment in a room filled with wood. One wall was lined with stacked timber that had been chopped and split, the other with various parts of trees. A roll-up garage door lead to a truck-sized entry from street level down to the basement. The windows in the door had been boarded over, inside and out, in the fashion of the windows in the upper floors.

In between the two piles of wood stood a chopping block for quartering wood and crumpled before it was the body of an old man, the ax still in his hand, a rifle not far away. The quartered pieces of a log lay scattered around the room.

"Looks like our timing is impeccable," Mia said. "No wonder this building has survived unmolested. He's been guarding it."

"Probably had a heart attack chopping wood," Christian said. "He hasn't been here all that long." He reached down, turning the man over and gently closing his eyes. He laid the man out respectfully, crossing his arms over his chest.

"It's cool down here, probably slowed the decay," she said. Then the smell got to her, and she fled the furnace room.

Christian walked past her into the laundry, and she followed. He pulled a couple of unadorned white sheets from the makeshift clothesline hung across the room and headed back to the old man. Mia remained in the laundry, breathing the clean air and steadying her stomach.

CHAPTER FIFTEEN

"I THINK we should tell people that he's still alive and has invited us to use the ballroom," Mia said. "That way no one will challenge our right to be there. Well, maybe not say he's still alive, that would be fishy, but just that we're distant cousins or something and he's invited us to stay. I bet he didn't go outside much once he had this place boarded up."

They hustled back to the library in the late afternoon sunlight. They were excited. They'd found an entire building, untouched by the looting, and with its tenancy recently vacated. The desire to move fast fueled them.

"We'll have to bury him by night then," Christian replied. "Otherwise, someone will be bound to see and comment."

"That's a given," Mia said. "Look, there they are."

Glen and Sally were sitting in the late day sun, chatting with a man who turned out to be Melvin.

Glen looked up as they approached. "There you are. I hoped you'd show up soon. Melvin just was telling us how his storehouse was raided, and his partner killed."

"That's awful!" Mia exclaimed. "Why would anyone do that? You're doing humanitarian work."

"It's the Koupe Tribinal," Melvin said. "It has to be. No one else cuts down people for no reason. Roger was totally blameless. All he did was guard the medical supplies and protect me. He was my friend." He looked downcast and tired. "I had to bury him. I couldn't just leave him there."

Mia put a hand on his shoulder, "I'm so sorry," she said. "That must have been awful."

"Yeah, it was. And then I had to walk all the way home, avoid a mugging, and barter half my stuff away to get free. It's been a hell of a night and a day."

"We've got some good news," Christian said. "We found a building where we can set up a clinic. It has lots of windows for natural light, plenty of space. And the only catch is that we have to bury the former tenant." He glanced at Melvin and realized what he'd said. "Sorry, Melvin, I wasn't thinking."

Melvin had his eyes closed and waved away the remark. "No problem," he said.

Sally jumped up. "Let's go see it before the sun goes down," she said, nearly dancing with excitement.

They gathered their supplies and Christian led them back the way he and Mia had come, cutting across the park, and taking them around the rear of the building. Christian pulled the key he'd removed from the dead man out of his pocket and opened the door that led into the museum kitchen. When everyone was in the loft and the door barred behind them, Mia skipped up the stairs in her excitement to show the others.

Glen, Sally, and Melvin were suitably impressed with the ballroom. It was indeed big enough to do everything they needed, the main problem being getting the severely injured up the stairs.

"Maybe we can use the rooms off the kitchen for people who are really badly hurt," Mia said. "It's not like we're really going to use that kitchen for cooking, there's one in the apartment for preparing meals."

"When we walked through, I noticed everything was antique," Sally said. "Is this whole place really a museum?"

"Pretty much," Christian said. "There's storage in the basement, and the ground floor of one wing is the apartment, but other than that it's pretty much a giant-ass museum."

"A giant-ass museum," Melvin echoed and laughed.

"Come on," Mia said. "I'll show it to you."

They took a quick tour, skimming through the rooms until they reached the apartment, where they spent a little more time. "One of us should move in here," Melvin said. "To keep an eye on the place."

"I think we all should move in here," Glen said. "There's plenty of room, and we could take turns keeping watch. You know once we get up and running all those people who come up the stairs to get treated are going to talk. It won't be long before the undesirables know what's here."

"Maybe we should treat everybody in the rooms off the kitchen," Sally said, "and leave the ballroom for a hospital ward, or just leave it empty? Maybe we are less of a target that way."

"Come on," Christian said. "It's time to show you the not very pleasant part. Although, I do think Melvin's going to be thrilled with the storage. I think there's enough room that you could use the basement instead of your warehouse, Melvin. That would solve a lot of problems."

"Still have to get the supplies into the city," Melvin said. "That's the hardest part. The Koupe Tribinal have checkpoints on the major roads in, and they'd simply stop and loot us."

"Something to figure out then," Glen said. "Because Christian's right, it would solve a lot of problems if our medical supplies were here."

They trouped down into the basement, where Melvin reacted as expected. He looked at the storage space and the repair shop, and just about stopped breathing. "If we could get past the roadblocks..." His voice trailed off, and Mia could see he was imagining all the good that could be done. They moved into the laundry room, past the furnace, and into the area Mia thought of as the woodshed. Only it really wasn't the shed at all, but a kind of garage.

The man was lying where they'd left him, covered with a sheet. Glen lifted a corner of the cloth and pulled it gently back from the man's face. "He's dead alright," Glen said, "and at first glance, it really does look like natural causes. Not that I suspected Christian or Mia of knocking off the old boy, but somebody else could have."

"It really just looked like he was cutting wood and his heart stopped," Mia said. "It's not like he was a young guy."

"No, well past his prime," Glen said. "And probably not cut out for such a physically demanding life. Where can we bury him?"

"I was thinking in the courtyard," Christian said. We need to do it in the dark, so nobody knows he's gone."

"And that matters why?" Glen asked.

"Because clearly, he'd been protecting this place," Mia said. "It's the only building we've seen without the windows all smashed in, vampire-looking people sleeping in it, or just totally trashed. See that shotgun over there? It was right next to his side. I think he carried it everywhere."

"I see," Glen said. "Was this really the only suitable building you came across?"

"Yeah, and we walked all day. And a couple of times we walked really quickly away," Christian said dryly.

"I can't say it's not excellent," Glen said. "More than big enough. Defendable. Easy deliveries." He pointed to the overhead door in the wall. "It's well decked out."

"That just leaves us to give this man a decent burial," Melvin said. "And for me to be extremely grateful to him for protecting this building. I think Christian and Mia are correct. If we can get our supplies delivered in town, this will be a more than satisfactory place to store them. I'll check with my delivery team."

They waited for dark in the apartment, heating canned goods on the propane stove. Melvin and Sally went down into the basement to see if they could get the fire going again and to see if there were ways to block off the vent, so they weren't heating the entire building. The ideal situation would be to warm the examining room near the kitchen, and the apartment. Then if they ever turned the ballroom into the hospital ward to heat that room as well. Although Glen did notice that the sun hitting the windows did create a certain amount of ambient warmth.

That was the main downfall of the kitchen wing, the sunlight did not hit the windows there, not nearly as long as it did up in the ballroom. It would not be as warm nor as light as the upper floor, but there was no denying it would be easier to contain their patients on the ground floor. He had images of children running through the halls and in and out of all the museum rooms. A lot of the women brought all their children with them, regardless if they needed treating or not. It would be so easy for the mothers to lose track of a child or two on the long climb. No, the kitchens really were a better location, unless they were to build stairs up the front of the house to the balcony. That hardly was feasible. He felt foolish even thinking about it.

He felt the hot air rising through the vents long before the men arrived back in the room. It had been so long since he'd had any kind of central heating it felt like a luxury. It was a luxury, he realized. In the history of human endeavor, central heating was a blip. Well, it was a blip he would enjoy the heck out of.

Finally, darkness fell, and they loaded the old man's body onto a dolly and wheeled him through the big overhead door and up onto the driveway. It was a good thing it was dark because then they had to wheel him around the apartment wing of the building into the courtyard. During daylight, there would have been no way to hide what they were doing.

Christian and Melvin had taken turns digging the grave in a neglected flower bed in the center of the courtyard. They had not asked Glen to help because he needed to save his hands for practicing medicine. Glen had objected, offering to take his turn, but they had voted him down. They all were relying on his skills to keep them alive, so he was spared the grunt work.

Christian and Melvin jumped down into the grave. Then Glen, Sally, and Mia handed down the corpse. He wasn't all that dense, mostly bone and skin, although there was a little bit of muscle there, probably acquired in the effort to maintain the building. Christian and Melvin laid him gently in the dirt and then scrambled up and out of the hole.

They just were starting to shovel dirt when they heard a noise. Sally spotted the cluster of children first and pointed. They didn't run when they were discovered but stood there gaping and whispering. Sally walked over to them.

"Are you spying on us?" she asked. "Because you really shouldn't spy on people. They may not like it, and something bad could happen to you."

"Will you kill us the way you killed him?" a boy of about twelve asked, pointing to where the others still were shoveling dirt.

"We didn't..." Sally began, but Melvin came up behind her and touched her shoulder, stopping her speech.

"Yes," Melvin said, "we will. We own this building now,

and if anybody bothers us, we'll run them off just like that old fellow did. Only there's more of us, and we are a lot meaner than him."

The group seemed to pull in on itself, shrinking together, becoming more cohesive. They took a few steps back. "What are you going to do here?" asked a high small trembling voice.

"See that man over there?" Melvin asked. "He's a doctor. We're going to use this building as a doctor's office for people who can't afford to pay the doctors in the hospitals. So when you get sick, you can come here, and we will try to make you better."

"I thought you said you were mean, that you'd run us off," a child said.

"And I will," Melvin said. "If I find you around here at night, or if I find you trying to get in any of the other doors, I will run you off. If I catch you, I'll beat you to within an inch of your life. Do you understand? You mess with us, we'll mess you up. But if you're sick or hurt and need help, you come to that door over there. Understand?"

There was some nodding and shuffling, and the group disappeared around the side of the building. There was a collective sigh of relief, and they resumed shoveling dirt back into the grave.

"I thought we weren't going to let anyone know the old man was dead," Sally said.

"That was the plan," Melvin said, "but we were spotted. Pretty soon everyone in a five-block radius is going to know that old man is dead, but they would've figured it out anyway. This way they think we killed him, which makes us tougher than him. And they're all going to hear through the grapevine that we're practicing medicine here."

"But so will the people who run the hospitals, won't they? We heard some awful stories about what happens to people who don't obey the Tribinal. At least that's what they call it. I thought they meant tribunal, but I guess not. It's Koupe Tribinal. Someone told me it was a Haitian phrase, he was a brown wrinkly old man. Probably Haitian himself, I'd guess." Sally stopped talking as she took the shovel from Mia to do her twenty shovelfuls.

"I think someone should stay here tonight," Mia said as they were finishing up by stamping the dirt down. "In case anyone comes snooping around. We can't bar the door if we aren't on the inside."

"You have a point," Glen said. "I can stay here."

"We'll need you to help carry the heavier items back," Melvin said. "No offense, but the women don't have the upper body strength that you have."

"If it comes to that," Sally said, "I'm the weakest, so I should stay behind. Now that there aren't any dead bodies in the house it won't be so creepy."

"Did we close the door into the wood storage area?" Mia asked, suddenly worried about seeing images of marauders running through the museum.

"It's closed and locked," Melvin said. "But we need to go back inside to bar it."

"Are we finished here?" Glen asked. "Good. Then let's go back in and secure the building before we leave. I want Sally to feel safe."

They trouped back in through the French doors, locking and barring them before heading to the basement to bar the overhead door. That door was trickier, because not only was the steel bar that ran across the entry long and heavy, there was also a wedge that blocked the top of the door to keep it from sliding upward.

"I don't know how that old man did this," Mia groaned from her perch on the ladder, which appeared to have been left next to the door for this purpose, "I can't steady myself on the ladder and lift this weight at the same time." The wedge was solid and really heavy. "Do you think it's lead?"

"Here, let me do it," Christian said from the bottom of the ladder. "Maybe he had the delivery guy come in and open the door for him. I don't think he could have lifted the bar either."

Mia made her way down the ladder, leaving the wedge balanced on the top of the door. "Be careful. If that thing falls on your head, you'll be dead before you know what hit you."

"You bet." Christian climbed the ladder, fixed the wedge in place and was back down in minutes. He dusted off his hands in triumph.

"Don't be a braggart," Mia said and then laughed. She was so happy they'd found this place. They'd have real heat, and apparently, the furnace could be used to supply hot water as well. There were benefits to finding a building that still had all its mechanical devices from before electricity.

They went from door to door as a group, making sure the building was secure, and then Sally walked them to the kitchen wing. Mia turned to her.

"Don't answer the door until we come back," Mia said. "I don't care what they say, don't open the door. The best idea is to go to bed in the apartment. I saw fresh sheets in the cupboard. Put in earplugs and sleep until morning. We won't be here first thing because we need to bring our stuff, plus a few things from your family's apartment, and then lock it up. But we'll be here before noon. Okay?"

"I'll be fine," Sally said. "But I don't know why one of us is staying if all we have to do is go to sleep."

"Because if anything is loud enough to wake you up," Christian put in, "then point the rifle in the direction of the noise and shoot. That should scare the worst of them away."

"A maniac with a rifle trumps a bad guy with a handgun," Melvin said. "Also, you can scream. There are still people in the city that come running when they hear a woman scream. Take advantage of that if you need to." He put a hand on her shoulder. "You'll be fine. People are used to leaving this building alone. They aren't likely to come looking in the night when they'll be at a disadvantage."

Sally nodded, and Mia hugged her. "Do you want me to stay too?" she asked. "They don't really need me."

"No, you go," Sally said. "I'll be fine. This place is trussed up like a fortress, and I'm not worried."

Well, I am, Mia thought to herself. *We really shouldn't split up like this.*

They left through the back entryway, Mia standing at the door until she heard all the locks click shut and the bar slide into place.

"It's locked up tight," Sally called through the door. "You can go."

"See you tomorrow," Mia called back, and the men shushed her. "Typical men," she muttered. "Don't know what's important and what's not."

They slipped around the side of the building, and when they had crossed the street and were moving through the park, Mia looked back. The moon was shining on the face of the building, and Sally was standing on the balcony, watching them go.

"Go back inside, you twit," Mia whispered to her. "Before Prince Charming tries to climb up there and claim you."

Then she turned and followed the men across the moonlit park.

CHAPTER SIXTEEN

Glen also noticed Sally standing outside. He questioned the judgment of leaving her there alone and almost turned back but decided against it because that might undermine her confidence. She was locked and barred into the place after all. He caught movement from the corner of his eye and turned to look forward. He scanned the street on the far edge of the park but saw nothing. This did not ease his concern but intensified it. Someone or something did not want to be spotted. That couldn't be good.

He trusted his instincts and knew that whatever he thought he'd seen was there somewhere, so he did not let down his guard. When the attack came, he was ready. Unfortunately, there were so many of them that being prepared wasn't enough. Three of them for every one of us, Glen thought, not good odds. Mia was emitting hair-raising cries and kicking out in every direction. That was good. She had five of them trying to subdue her, reducing the number the rest of them had to fight. As he watched, one of them grabbed her from behind, a mistake on their part as she used the person to take her weight as she kicked higher and caught another of the attackers in the face with her boot heel.

A stocky man came at Glen, and he had to focus on the task at hand, leaving his admiration for Mia for another time. The man swung a fist, and Glen ducked, going down on one knee and them back up again, using his momentum to launch himself into the man's gut. Which was like hitting a rock wall with his shoulder. The man didn't move and brought both fists down together on Glen's back.

He went down hard, and his assailant rolled him over and brought a boot down on his face. He felt the man going through his pockets and growling when he didn't find anything. They'd left their backpacks full of medical supplies at the museum. They literally didn't have anything worth stealing.

Of course, that didn't stop the assailant from breaking his nose. The blood was running down the back of his throat, making him gag. He rolled onto his side and received a boot in the kidney. But at least he wouldn't drown in the blood he was about to vomit up.

He opened his eyes to see Melvin rolled into a ball protecting his gut with his arms, his cheek tucked into his shoulder as two men kicked him in turns. He must have taken a pretty heavy blow to his stomach to be leaving his head unprotected, and it occurred to Glen that they all might die here.

Another kick to his kidney left him gasping, and he was going to try crawling away, a hopeless gesture, he knew, but he couldn't just lie here and let them kill him. He just was gathering together the strength to roll onto his hands and knees when a rifle blast split the night. Then another.

He heard Sally yell, "Take that you bastards," and another shot rang out. The man who'd been kicking Glen fell to the ground behind him, which Glen thought was a smart move if he wanted to stay alive, but when he rolled to look, Glen saw he was dead. The back of his skull was blown away.

The thugs who were fortunate enough still to be alive took off running, leaving their dead and wounded behind. Sally shot at them as they ran, hitting at least one of them. Sally set down the rifle and went to Melvin, murmuring quietly to him. Then she checked on each of the rest of them, coming to Glen last.

"I think we need to get Melvin and Christian back to the museum," she said. "Do you think you can walk?"

"I probably can walk," he said, "but I'm not up to carrying anybody."

"I've got that covered. I'm leaving the gun here with you, and I'll be back in a minute." She left the rifle within his reach and took off running across the park. People were watching now, the gunfire had lured them out of their safe spaces, but no one seemed to be approaching.

As Sally reached the far sidewalk, a small figure approached her. They stood talking for a moment, then the child ran off down the street, and Sally disappeared behind the museum. She was back a minute later with what looked like a giant piano dolly with a handle. It bumped over the grass and stopped. Sally swore, took the dolly back to the sidewalk and pulled it around to the walkway closest to where Glen and the others were lying on the ground.

Mia got up and met Sally next to Melvin. Between them, they were able to get him up off the ground and support him over to the dolly, where he lay curled on his side again. Glen was going to have to get up and examine him. It was clear Melvin was hurt much worse than he was. Glen set about sitting up, rolling onto his side first and then levering himself up. By the time he was sitting the girls had Christian on the dolly with Melvin.

"It will take us a little while to get him home," Sally said. "Follow when you feel up to it. And don't forget the rifle."

The rifle was there at his knee, but he hadn't paid it much attention. "What about this body? We can't just leave it here, can we?" Glen asked. He wished his face didn't hurt so bad. His nose was broken for sure. Other than that, he didn't know what damage there was. Except that it hurt like hell. He had a headache too, but that seemed tolerable compared to his face.

"The cleaners will come and get it," Melvin said. "Just leave it."

As he limped across the green to the museum, he wondered how Sally felt about killing a man. Would she spend days crying over it, or did it not matter to her? Had she killed in the battle back in New Town? He couldn't remember.

Blood from his nose was soaking his shirtfront, and he half wished he'd gotten on and rode back with the other men. Were the women stronger, or had they not been hurt as badly? Or woman, Sally hadn't been in the fight. His head was fuzzy, and he stopped to sit on a bench for a few minutes.

He woke up in a bed with Sally bending over him and a searing pain in his nose.

"Oh, good," she said. "You're awake. I set the nasal bone as best I could, but I think you may have fractured cheekbones as well. Can I do anything about those? Should I?"

He felt his face, which was bruised and swelling. "Nothing seems out of place," he said. "Better leave it. How are the others?"

"Christian has an injured ankle. There's no way to know if it's broken or sprained. Other than that just bruises mostly. My best guess for Melvin is some kidney damage, but I need you to tell me what it is, and what we need to do. He's the one I'm most worried about. Mia gave worse than she got.

Her wrists and ankles are bruised and scraped. They kept trying to keep her still, and she kept resisting. She's good at using her body as a weapon."

"How do you feel about the man who died?" he asked softly.

She looked at him in surprise. "That worthless piece of humanity? I'd shoot him again without hesitation. All of them for that matter. I see no reason why they should be allowed to live. Assholes."

Well then, no problem there, Glen thought, and definitely no tears. These girls were tough.

He started to get up, got dizzy and laid back down. "I think it's going to take me a few minutes to get vertical," he said. "If I try going too fast, I'll just pass out again."

"I've got Melvin comfortable in the room across the hall. I think it must have been the old butler's office. There are some clean clothes here," she indicated a pile on a chair and left the room.

Glen looked around and realized he hadn't be laid in a bed after all. Sally had found a mattress and laid it on the dining room table. The chairs had been shoved in on one side of the table, perhaps to keep him from rolling off. On the other side, they'd been pushed against the wall. It was one of these chairs that held the pile of clean clothes.

He swung his legs over the edge of the table and sat for a while. It turned into a long while as his head swam and dots flashed in front of his eyes. Eventually, his head stopped trying to kill him, and he was able to stand and even change his clothes. He stepped carefully across the hall, not trusting his brain to keep him upright, and thought about what he knew about kidneys. He was a brain surgeon, not an internal organs guy, but as he was all Melvin had. He had better get his act together.

Melvin was conscious but in pain and sweating. Glen sat

in a chair next to his bed, which was a mattress on a large desk. He'd have to ask Sally where she found the spare mattresses when he had a free moment.

"You don't look so good, Doc," Melvin said. "Maybe you should go back to bed."

"I'm doing better than you are, medic, so save your energy. Tell me where you hurt." Glen leaned forward, trying to get comfortable, but the thing is that when your face hurts there is no better position.

Melvin told him what had happened, where he hurt and what he thought the diagnosis was: a bruised kidney. Glen examined his back, felt around a little, and agreed.

"You could have just agreed to begin with and left off the poking around," Melvin said a little breathlessly. "Rest and fluids?"

"Rest, fluids and antibiotics," Glen said, "as a precaution. If that kidney is torn, we might stave off an infection. Bed for a week."

"But our move," Melvin said.

"Can wait," Glen answered. "You are to stay in bed. Now I have to go see Christian. Apparently, he has a twisted/broken ankle."

"I have a boot back at the apartment," Melvin said. "It's in the hall closet."

"I'll keep that in mind. Now, rest. I'll have Sally bring you something for the pain."

"Not a narcotic. I've got a tendency to get addicted." Melvin looked embarrassed. "It's hereditary."

"One pill, just to get you through tonight, er, today," the sun was coming up. "Then I'll put you on over-the-counter painkillers. Okay? So you can sleep."

"One dose. That's all I'll take." Melvin set his mouth.

"That's all I'll ask you to take. I'll check in later." Glen stepped out into the hall and leaned against the wall. That little examination had taken every bit of energy he had. Mia came around the corner and saw him, speeding up to clasp his arm and help him back into the dining room.

"That's enough walking around for you," she said. "How's Melvin?"

"He needs antibiotics and a dose of whatever narcotic we have on hand." Glen sat on the bed, table, whichever, and closed his eyes. "I need the same. Then I've got to look at Christian."

"We've got Christian under control," Mia said. "Sally has his leg elevated. There's no way to know if it's broken or a soft tissue injury."

"Melvin has a walking cast back at the apartment, in the closet," Glen said. "I don't know if it will fit him or not, but it's worth a try when you can't keep him in bed anymore."

"I'll get it this afternoon," Mia said. "You lie down, and I'll get the meds the doctor prescribed."

"What doctor?" he asked, confused.

"Boy, you are in bad shape." She rolled her eyes. "You. You are the doctor, dumbass. Get in bed."

He laid down, and she slipped his shoes off for him and covered him with a blanket. She woke him up five minutes later to give him the meds, and he was asleep again almost instantly.

Mia let Sally do the bulk of the nursing and spent the next few days doing errands for her. It wasn't that she was an inadequate nurse, it's just that Sally was so much better at it that she was. It was the second day that Sally came to her.

"Do we have supplies at the apartment? I really could use more bandages and adhesive tape." Sally said.

"Let me ask," Mia said, and went in search of Melvin, who was sitting in the sun relaxing.

"Are there any medical supplies back at the apartment?"

she asked him. "Sally says we're low on bandages and adhesive."

"Sure," he said, "but I'll need to tell you where they are hidden. I didn't like to leave supplies where they easily could be looted. I never had a problem, but you never know, and getting those supplies wasn't easy. You know, I went through fifteen bicycles bringing those supplies back from the supply house."

"You lost bikes?" Mia asked. "How did that happen?"

"Mostly I had to ditch them to get away from freeway robbers," he said. "Sometimes I'd go over a fence, or through a water pipe. Couldn't take the bike with me. The bikes always were gone when I made it back. So I guess the robbers got something."

"But at least you got away," Mia said.

"Yeah, at least I got away." Melvin smiled. "Let me tell you where to find what you need. There's a vent fan in the ceiling, it flips down. In the duct, there are things like bandages and medical scissors. In the main bedroom, there is a false panel in the back of the closet on the right. You'll have to move the shoe rack. Then, in the kitchen, slide the microwave out of its mount and look behind. You'll find more things there."

Mia went to find Sally. "Hey Sal, the answer is yes, we have supplies. I'll go get them. Melvin has them hidden all over the apartment."

"Are we doing the right thing, Mia?" Sally asked, suddenly serious. "We left safety to come here. But my blood ran cold when I saw them beating on you in the park. What would I do if I lost you? I'd be all alone."

"We found Melvin, didn't we? If we lose each other, we'll find others. Like attracts like, you won't be alone. But we'll get smarter, I promise. I'll do everything I can to always come back to you. I'll always come back."

Sally burst into tears.

Mia put her arm around Sally and pulled her close. "You cry, Sal. It's surprising we aren't all crying every day. Our whole lives have changed, but you've adapted. You've learned how to help people, how to give to society instead of taking. That's a lot. It's big. And it's worth crying over. When I cry, it's because I haven't figured out what to do yet. I'm just a drain on what little civilization that's left. But you? You're valuable. I will be here for you whenever I can."

Sally sniffed and ran her sleeve across her eyes. "What do you mean you're a drain?" she asked. "You're part of our team. You help keep us going. What could Glen or I do without you and Christian to take care of scouting out locations and taking watch? Just because you don't put Band-aids on boo-boos doesn't mean you aren't valuable."

"But I don't have a calling, Sal," Mia said sadly. "Anyone could do what I'm doing now. I want to contribute in a more... not valuable, but maybe more satisfying way. I don't want to be a grunt. I want to be a specialist. And I will, I just haven't found my specialty yet. But I will. Just like you have."

"I didn't really find it, it found me," Sally said. "Glen needed help, and I found I could do what was needed. And then I realized I enjoyed helping. Taking the lesser injuries, just like a mother would, I think. Like my mom when I'd cut myself or fall. She'd clean me up and slap a bandage over the hurt spot and give me a kiss. That's what I'm doing so that Glen can take the difficult cases. The split heads and broken bones. Infections and diseases. Only I'm not giving everyone kisses, only the children." She smiled as if in memory. "Only there were one or two young men I wouldn't have minded kissing."

Mia frowned. "Does it bother you that I'm with Christian now?" she asked. "I'm sure you'll find someone too. What about Melvin?"

"Melvin is devoted to his cause. I don't think he even

looks at women as potential partners. And anyway he's too old for me. I want someone closer to my age, and maybe just a little handsome. But don't get me wrong, character comes first."

"So, not Glen then, if age is an issue," Mia said and grinned.

"No!" Sally cried. "My god, Mia, he's old enough to be my father."

"Some women like older men," Mia said. "Sugar daddies."

"Ew. Yuck. No, thank you. Young men are bad enough, I don't want one who is all old and wrinkled." Sally pulled a face.

"Wait," Mia's eyes grew wide. "Are we talking penises here? Because I don't think Glen's would be wrinkly."

"Mia! Shut up. No, we aren't talking, um, private parts, we're talking faces. And Glen isn't really old enough to be my dad, but he feels kind of like an older brother. I have no interest in seeing him undressed. Just, no."

Sally's face was so scrunched up that Mia just had to laugh. And then run away as Sally pitched things at her.

She made trips to the apartment to fetch supplies in the company of Robbie, a ten-year-old street urchin who'd befriended Sally the day they'd been attacked in the park.

She felt marginally safer going out with Robbie than on her own. He wasn't a big ten-year-old, but he was scrappy, and he knew the areas to stay away from. He also was handy as a pack animal, and carried supplies back from the apartment.

At first, she was worried he might spread the word to his friends, and they'd come back one day to find out the apartment had been looted or was filled with pre-teens, but as that hadn't happened, she had to assume he hadn't said a word to anyone. They traveled back and forth, sometimes two and three times a day, always taking a different route and checking to see no one had followed them before scooting through the fence at the back of the apartment building.

One day, they were on their way back with a particularly valuable haul when Robbie stopped short and hissed, Can't go that way, follow me," and ducked down an alley. They were two-thirds of the way from the next street when a looming shadow appeared. Mia risked a glance behind. There was someone there too. Two buildings, and...

Panic had begun making her heart beat faster when a hand reached out and pulled her through an arched entryway to a courtyard. Robbie was there before her, standing with the tall woman who'd grabbed her. The door to the yard was slammed shut and bolted.

The woman motioned her to follow, then led them across the entryway and through a doorway into a building. It was dark, cool, and eerily silent. The only noise was coming from her hiking boots as she walked the tile floor. The woman wore a kind of moccasin, and Robbie's sneakers also made no sound.

They moved through a maze of hallways lit only by a glow stick the women pulled from a pocket, turning this way and that in the eerie green light until Mia lost all sense of direction. They went through an opening that had been knocked through the wall between the buildings. Now they were walking on worn carpeting, and her footfalls were silent as well.

Considering the route they were taking couldn't be more than a square block long, it seemed to be taking them a long time. Mia's head had begun hurting from straining her eyes to see if there were any markings on the doors or walls that would indicate where they were. There were occasional signs, but nothing she could read in the dim light, beyond the EXIT or floor signs. They descended a stairwell down into a basement and moved through a cavernous space into what looked like a hand-dug tunnel. It was claustrophobic. Mia sucked in air and tried to steady her heart. Then they were through it and into another building, going up the stairs. When they finally exited they were across the park from the museum, having walked the remainder of their trip through dark buildings.

Mia was nervous about leaving what felt like the safety of the building out onto the street, but the woman motioned her out with both hands, using a quaint sweeping motion. Mia reluctantly followed Robbie onto the road, and when she turned back to thank the woman, she already was gone.

"That was the quietest person I've ever met," Mia said, following Robbie across the street. "Is silence crucial in there?"

"Her tongue's been cut out," Robbie said, "She can't speak. But she's a good guide."

"Her tongue was cut out! Why?" Mia was outraged and slightly sickened by the thought.

"That happens to people who know too much about the Koupe Tribinal." He shrugged. "That's why most of us stay far away."

"And how did she know to help us when we were trapped in the alleyway?"

"There are many such places around town," he said. "A group of people watches them on a rotation. Sometimes they get shut down by the Tribinal, sometimes by other people. But when that happens, a new one will crop up somewhere nearby. There's always been one in that alley."

"But don't days go by when no one needs help?" She was trotting and a little breathless now with trying to talk and keep up with him.

"People don't use them just when they are in trouble. Lots of people use them to move across town. It's far safer, and the people of the Tribinal can't follow you. The less those people know about you, the better."

They reached the museum and went around back. Mia stopped Robbie with a hand.

"Pretty soon we'll go back to our apartment to bring the rest of the things that we need back here," she said. "When we do, I want you to stay here and keep an eye on the museum for us. When we leave you can bar the door, and you'll be perfectly safe, but also the museum will be safe with you here to protect it. Can you do that for me?"

Robbie frowned. "I think it would be better for me to come with you. That way I can lead you to the safe places when the bad people come after you. Alice could watch the museum. She knows how to fire a gun."

Now Mia frowned. "It's not safe for you to come with us, Robbie. People don't like what we're doing, and they keep sending thugs after us. I don't want you to be caught in that. What if we couldn't get to a safe place in time? You could be killed. I don't want that for you."

"But if I'm with you, you are less likely to be caught," Robbie countered. "The people in the safe places know me. If I'm not with you, they may not let you through. You need the supplies to help people, so you need me to help get them here." His face showed a stubborn determination.

It was not going to be easy to convince him to stay behind, Mia thought. But it seemed necessary to keep him safe. Her own Artful Dodger. Not a thief, but their guide and the leader of the neighborhood children.

She'd have to find out more about those children once they were set up. Did they have homes, families? Or were they living on the street with only Robbie to keep them safe and fed, out of the cold and away from the people who would steal them away? She had no doubt there were plenty of people who gladly would sell the children into slavery if they were able.

If they were homeless, she'd have to see they were housed in the museum. There was plenty of room. They could go to school here, keep the knowledge from dying. In fact, even if they had homes and families, there should be a school here. Medicine and learning together in one place. She and Christian could be in charge of the school. She smiled. Now she knew what her job would be, and it was satisfying. She had a purpose.

But for now, she needed to convince Robbie to stay. "Listen, Robbie, you've got to think about your responsibilities. Your posse relies on you. What if you weren't able to make it back to them? What would they do? They'd be lost without you."

"Alice would take over," he said stubbornly. "You can't leave me behind, or you can, but I won't stay. I'll follow you anyway. So you might as well let me help."

"I don't think Glen will let you come," she said. "He wants you to be safe too. And you'd be helping, keeping the things we have here safe. You'd be our sentry."

His demeanor changed abruptly. "Okay," he said. "I'll make sure your stuff here stays safe. Can we go in now?"

"Yeah, I guess so." But somehow she felt she'd lost that argument, even though he'd given in.

They went in, dropping their loot in the entryway, and walked through to the museum kitchen. Sally, Glen, Melvin, and Christian were sitting at the big wood plank farm kitchen table playing cards.

"Who is winning?" Mia asked.

"Melvin, of course." Christian sounded disgusted. "He's got the best poker face of anyone I've ever met."

"We've decided we're tired of hanging around," Melvin said. "We want to do a final run on the apartment tomorrow, get everything necessary out and lock it up tight."

"Are you well enough to do a walk like that?" she asked Glen. "Or is that going to set you back? We have lines of people here every day hoping to get treated. Sally and I are doing our best, but the sickest people really need you guys."

"Everyone is recovered sufficiently to make the walk across town, although Christian will have to wear the boot." Glen gestured toward the plastic cast sitting off to one side of the table. "We can see people in the morning and do the walk in the early evening. We need to be back before dusk falls."

"Whatever you say, mine Capitan," Mia shot Glen a mock salute.

"Oh quit," he said. "We all came up with the plan. It wasn't just me."

"Mine spokesman, then," she said and ducked out of the way when he crumpled a piece of paper and threw it at her.

They were worn out the next day when they left for the apartment. Mia not much more than usual, but the men had worked a full day for the first time since moving to the museum, and their weariness showed. Still, they insisted on making the trip, not wanting to put it off yet another day.

"I'll be even more tired tomorrow evening," Christian said. "Might as well take care of it now."

Mia felt some trepidation as they started across the park. It was broad daylight, she reminded herself, there was no need to worry. But she remembered the figures who had trapped Robbie and herself during the day in the alleyway the day before and was not reassured.

The trip to the apartment was uneventful. They stopped twice to rest, letting Christian ease his leg a few minutes, and Melvin adjust the support he wore around his torso. The apartment building seemed the same as the day before, although Mia was alarmed when an older man on the first floor saw them, slid back into his home and slammed and locked the door.

She looked around to gauge the others' reactions to this, but no one else seemed to have noticed. She shrugged it off. And when they walked into the apartment, it appeared her fears where pointless. Everything looked the same as always, certainly the same as yesterday. They surged into the living room and plopped down on the couches and chairs with sighs of relief.

"I'll miss this furniture," Sally was saying, but she was cut off when a large man entered the room from the kitchen.

He was tall and broad, well-muscled and in good health. There was no shortage of protein and carbs in this man's life as he radiated well-being. The corners of Mia's mouth turned down. Only the bad guys looked as healthy as this. On top of that, he was sporting a wolfish grin.

"Where is Melvin Foles?" he asked.

"I've never heard of Melvin Foles," Melvin said. "You must have the wrong apartment."

"You're lying," the man said. "This is Melvin Foles' apartment. Where is he?"

"I don't know what you are talking about," Sally said and nodded toward Mia. "This is Mia's mother's apartment. They've owned this apartment for as long as Mia has been alive."

Mia nodded in agreement, even though Sally wasn't a hundred percent correct. What did details matter in this situation?

"Here," she said, rising and pulling open a drawer in a side table. "This is a picture of us."

The thug waved the picture away. "That doesn't mean one of you isn't Melvin Foles," he said.

"What do you want with Melvin Foles?" Christian asked. "Did he diss your sister?"

"Don't be silly, nobody would dare mess with a girl with a brother like that," Sally said.

"Maybe he didn't know," Glen said. They were all playing for time, trying to see a way out of this mess.

"Or maybe Melvin's a she," Mia said. "Short for Melvina. Maybe Melvina dumped his sister, and he's out to get her now."

"I'm not out to get Melvina, I mean Melvin," the man said. "And you don't want to mess with the people who are looking for him. If you won't tell me who Melvin Foles is, then I will take you all with me." He reached behind him and pulled a machine gun holstered on his back. Mia didn't know anyone actually really kept their guns there.

"Wait," Mia cried. "I'm Melvin, I'll go with you." She didn't know why she would sacrifice herself for the real Melvin Foles, and she was scared shitless, but she did know it was the right thing to do.

"Sorry, Melvin," he said, stressing the name, "but you waited too long. I'm taking you all. Get up." He waved his gun at the others who still were sitting on the couches. "Get a move on."

They got up slowly, all feigning more significant injuries than they had, and pushed the limits of his patience until he raised the machine gun and threatened to shoot Sally if they didn't get a move on. They moved.

Out on the street, Mia saw Robbie standing across the street looking worried. She put her hand behind her back and shooed him away. He started shaking his head no. She glowered at him and mouthed 'go away' while the thug who had them at gunpoint was looking the other way. Robbie looked stricken and slunk away, looking dejected. Mia felt a sigh of relief. The last thing her conscience needed was a child being hauled away with them.

They were herded down the street, people keeping well

out of their way. No one offered to help, but neither did they jeer at them. They just held a creepy silent vigil as the group passed. Once or twice, Mia tried reaching a woman with her eyes, but everyone looked away, pretending not to see her, or apologizing with their eyes, while giving her a barely perceptible shake of the head.

Sally reached out her hands in supplication when they passed close to a family, but the woman gathered her children close as her partner stepped in front of them, a look of stern disapproval on his face. 'I understand your need, but I cannot help you, and you have no right to ask," was written on his expression, a clear reprimand.

A child who Mia recognized as one they had treated started crying and went to Sally only to be thrust away by the thug. She fell, tearing her pants on the curb, now crying harder. A woman dashed across the street and gathered her in her arms, carrying her away while quietly admonishing her. Mia's heart went out to the child. She only had wanted to help Sally because Sally had been kind and now she had been punished for it.

Finally, they turned down a deserted side street and then an empty alley until they came to a set of stairs leading down to a door with torches burning on both sides and a sinister grinning jackal above it. The Koupe Tribinal, Mia thought. It's what she expected, but she'd been hoping she was wrong. Any other bad guy in this city would be preferable to the Cut Court, from what she'd heard.

They were practically pushed down the stairs to the jackal-adorned door at the bottom. Mia watched as Glen felt for the gun he'd slid into his waistband at his back and wondered if he could take this guy before he opened the door. But it was a moot point because the door opened of its own accord.

CHAPTER SEVENTEEN

THEY WERE PUSHED into a passageway and then into a cavernous room where they were shoved to their knees. Sally cried out in pain and Glen gritted his teeth. He hated the brutality of these people. Whatever it was that Melvin had done to piss off these people, they had to know Sally was innocent of it. And yet they felt the need to manhandle them all.

He wondered which of the men they thought Melvin was. Perhaps not Christian as he was likely too young, but, yes, they must know it was one of the other two of them. Glen began making a plan for when all hell broke loose. First, he must get the women out of here. Mia would say that was chivalrous bullshit, but it was the way he was raised. Protect the innocent. Save the injured from further harm. Heal if you could.

The room was cold, but still, the odor in the place was overwhelming. Coppery and nausea-inducing. He hated to think what it would be like if the room were warm. He began breathing through his mouth, but it was there on his tongue, sharp and unpleasant. It was reminiscent of an odor he knew well. Blood. It was an odor all surgeons knew well. But this wasn't fresh blood. He put the thought from his mind. He must focus.

His eyes roamed the cavernous room for possible escape routes. It had been made to look like a cave, with a raised dais spanning the far end. The stone wall behind the dais was oddly shaped, curved faintly, rounding the room, but the edges appeared not to be connected to the side walls, which made Glen think there was a passage into the chamber. There was the door they'd entered through, but without turning around, he could not tell what was behind him. The door had been on the side of the room. He didn't have a sense of how deep the room was.

Could there be another exit back there? When he saw his chance, he'd attempt to look around, but at the moment the assumption had to be that the gun still was pointed at Sally. He had no doubt the man holding it would shoot her for an infraction by one of her companions. It was the only thing that was keeping any of them in check. He could feel the tension running through all of them as they waited for a chance to turn the tables on their captors.

The handgun still was at his back. Either they had not noticed it there, or they didn't care that he had it. He hoped it was not the latter. If they knew he had a gun, and he made a motion that seemed as if he was reaching for it, whether he was or not, the man holding the machine gun would mow them down. Of *that*, he had no doubt.

He felt the presence of more people, possibly two or three more, entering the room and standing behind them. This would make an escape even more difficult. Escape around the dais then. Perhaps the people coming from the back did not feel the need to be armed, and they could just push them out of the way.

He heard Mia gagging next to him, and he shot his eyes to

the right. She was choking back vomit, he was sure of it. But why? His eyes scanned the floor in front of her and spotted the stain. Now he knew where the smell was coming from. An entire body's worth of blood had dried into a sticky pool. No wonder it smelled so bad in here. And soon there would be vomit too. Mia would not be able to hold it in for much longer. Why hadn't they cleaned it up? The room stunk enough like death without the physical remnants of what had happened here. Maybe they had left it for Melvin. They apparently liked to terrify their captives. Why not leave the evidence of what had happened to the last supplicant here? But then why didn't they leave the body as well? Surely that would be even more terrifying?

Perhaps the smell of decaying flesh on top of drying blood was too much even for the Court.

Mia retched and vomited, and Christian followed suit. When Sally and Melvin did not, he realized they, like himself, had had enough exposure to blood and vomit for it not to affect them. Medical professionals were accustomed to the worst of bodily odors. He kept his smile to himself. There were benefits to overexposure, but he was the last person to lord it over his friends.

A man appeared with a bucket and tossed fresh sawdust over the blood and two piles of vomit, filling the air with the smell of cedar. It was a welcome relief, even to Glen, and he saw Mia gasping, pulling in the fresh smelling air. In fact, all of them were breathing more deeply, and would as long as the cedar masked the smell of decay, blood and vomit.

His knees began hurting, and he wondered how long their captors intended to leave them here, waiting. Did they expect their prisoners to turn into blithering idiots if they left them waiting long enough? He took a sideways glance in both directions, but his companions seemed steady enough. Good. He would need them to be steady if they were to get out of this alive. And then they'd probably need to leave the city.

The Koupe Tribinal would not let them live in Detroit if they escaped. They probably should head far from here. Perhaps back to Philadelphia or as far away as San Francisco. It wouldn't matter where they went, they would be needed. Detroit would not be the only place where the poor were in desperate need of medical help.

The torches on the walls sputtered as a breeze swept through the room. Someone had opened the door. But still, no one appeared on the dais. Glen felt the pain in his knees spur his anger. He hated these tactics. Either kill us and have it done with or sit down like ordinary people and talk out the issue. The effort to demoralize him was wasted, and it was time he could spend helping people.

He thought again of the gun at his back. How many of them were there? The man with the gun, the man with the bucket, and at least two others. How many of the others were armed? If he faked fainting and rolled, he might be able to take out the one with the machine gun, but how many others?

None of his people were armed, leaving any gunfire strictly to him, but could Christian take a man down with his leg in a cast? If he could manage to convey the message to the others, would they know what to do? Would their legs even work after all this kneeling? He doubted his would.

"How long do you intend on keeping us here?" Melvin asked. "We've done nothing wrong."

"Quiet!" said the man with the machine gun.

"I will not remain quiet until I have an answer." Melvin's voice projected an edge that Glen never had heard. "What will it be, one hour, two, three?"

On three Glen began his fall. He spotted movement from either side but concentrated on yanking the gun from his pants as he rolled from his right side onto his back. But when he came to a stop on his back, his gun hand pointed up to where he thought the machine gun-weilding man should be, the stock end of the machine gun smacked him squarely in his broken nose and sent a rush of pain and dizziness through him. He felt, rather than saw, the firearm being torn from his hand.

There were noises of a struggle, but he couldn't bring himself to open his eyes. The pain in his face was excruciating, and he knew who would win this struggle. He heard the grunt as Mia hit the ground, a groan from Christian, and silence from the other two. Their bid for freedom had failed. He guessed it had been doomed to fail from the start, but they had to try. They couldn't go down without a fight.

He tasted blood. He wiped it from his face with the back of his sleeve. Gingerly, he put his fingers to his nose, checking the extent of the damage. The thug had been surprisingly gentle. He had tapped rather than smashed the broken nose. He hadn't inflicted further damage. The thug hadn't needed to tap hard, Glen's busted nose was enough to leave him incapacitated by the pain. He became aware of a burning sensation at his back and realized the gun had scraped the skin at his waistline. Nothing but an irritant compared to the pain in his face.

He lay there a few more minutes, breathing through his nose as the blood ran down his cheeks and into his ears. He must have looked like a mess. He certainly felt like a mess. There was a rustling and movement beside him. He cracked his eyes open to see a woman kneeling next to him, a cloth in her hand.

She dipped the cloth into a bowl on the floor and went to wash his face, but he put his hand up.

"Let me sit up first." He struggled into a semi-upright position, which made his ears ring and his head pound, but he held himself still as the woman began cleaning the blood from his face. She was thorough, swabbing the entirety of his ears and behind his neck where the blood still dripped. She held a cloth to his nostrils and went to pinch the bridge of his nose, but he made a noise of protest.

"Let me do it," he said. "It's broken."

She took her hand away and let him pinch his own throbbing nose. She finished wiping him down, shook her head, and went away muttering about brutality.

The others were released by their captors and sat up by degrees, where they were left for a few minutes of reprieve. Glen's head gradually stopped throbbing, and his nose stopped dripping blood. He tossed the bloody rag onto the pile of cedar shavings and felt his nose again. Swollen, but not further damaged he thought.

There was a rustle from behind the dais, and their guards prodded them back onto their knees. They were sloppy now, hurting, not the uptight angry people they were just a few moments before. There was a subtle shift in the attitudes of the people behind them, and even Melvin straightened up as three people appeared on the dais.

The first was a tall black woman dressed predominately in black, with tall boots and a long pistol on her thigh. She wore a necklace of large orange and green beads, and a scarf of the same colors around her head, partially corralling her hair. Over it all, she wore a judge's robe, open in the front. She sat regally in the center chair looking directly at the back of the room.

The man who followed was a younger black man, tall and lean with a shaved head. Under his robes he wore light colored chinos and a button-down shirt, accenting his youth. He crossed to the far side of the dais and sat in the chair set slightly back from the woman.

The third judge was a Caucasian man with short cut black

hair and a strange mask over his face, almost like a jester's or Punch's mask, only painted in darker colors with odd symbols on the cheeks. His robes were closed, making him look wizard-like. Glen thought it was about emotional control. This man was about generating fear with anonymity and this ugly façade. He would be cruel and unyielding. He sat stiff and upright in the chair closest to where they had entered the stage.

The three judges sat silent, seemingly looking into space, making them wait, and trying to break their nerve. Glen hated that kind of emotional bullshit. They could try unmanning him, but it wouldn't work. He was worried about the others, though. He shot a look toward Mia, but she looked steady, her jaw set. He couldn't see Christian beyond her, but Sally on his other side also looked firm. She was watching the man in the mask through slotted eyes. She had his number as well.

Good. Well then, assholes, bring it on. Glen straightened up. He may be battered, but he was not broken. They could make them wait as long as they wanted but it wasn't going to change a thing about how he responded. He didn't like bullies, and these were the worst kind of bully, using their power to cow the people around them.

The room was silent, and a tremor of energy was in the air. Glen breathed and waited. He saw Sally do the same, taking deep inhalations to remain calm. Their breath was visible since the room was so cold. Could their captors be cooling it down somehow? Another trick to disarm them? The three judges also left clouds in the air as they breathed. Finally, the woman stood, dominating the center of the dais with her physical presence, all eyes fixed on her alone.

Again they waited until she spoke:

"Who is Melvin Foles?

CHAPTER EIGHTEEN

MIA WAS EMBARRASSED by her reaction to the blood on the floor. She noticed it hadn't make Sally gag, but then Sally had been helping Glen for a while. She was used to blood. Except it wasn't just the sharp odor and the taste of copper in her mouth, it was also the amount of blood that was drying on the floor. Enough blood that it was clear that whoever had bled there also had died. Had probably been executed. It was that thought that had sent her over the edge. She'd been unable to stop her bile from rising.

She hated that she'd vomited in front of the thugs who had brought them here. The fact that Christian also had thrown up mollified her somewhat. In her mind, the objective was to get Melvin out of here alive. Then if they had to leave the city, well, that's what they would do. It wasn't as if anything was holding them here. Yes, they were needed, but they'd be welcomed anywhere they went. She didn't question why she had given her loyalty so wholly to a man she had known just a week or two.

He'd been helping people on his own for years. She was glad he'd found her family's apartment, and settled in there.

They'd discovered him there, and he hadn't chased them away but instead had welcomed them. He had so much in common with their group he fit right in, a natural addition to their mission.

For a brief moment, she wondered if they were right to leave the cabin in the woods. They'd been safe there, had allies in New Town. But she pushed that thought from her mind. Regrets wouldn't do anyone any good. They had to survive the current situation and get far, far away.

When Melvin began his countdown, she'd been ready and had launched herself onto an unarmed guard. He'd been twice her size, but she'd gotten her arm locked around his neck and had hung on for dear life, but he'd flipped her off, and she'd had the air knocked out of her when she'd hit the ground. She'd looked around when she'd finally been able to draw breath again to find they all were on the ground and Glen's nose still was bleeding.

She couldn't regret that they'd tried to get free, but she was hurting now, not starting from a place of power. Well, they'd just have to be smarter if they weren't stronger. She noticed Glen's gun was on the ground just behind the man with the firearm that looked to her like a machine gun. Maybe it was. Perhaps that's why they only needed one of their guards to be armed. He could mow them all down in a second.

When the three judges arrived on the stage Mia immediately dismissed the woman as cruel, the man in the mask as manipulative and probably also brutal. However, the younger man on the end closer to her was worried, she could see it in his eyes. This was a man with a conscience. If anyone could help them, it would be him. The man with compassionate eyes.

When the silence finally was broken, it was the woman who spoke. She stood straight, accentuating her height, which Mia noticed she enhanced with boots sporting at least four-inch heels. The psychological advantage. "Who is Melvin Foles?" she asked.

Again they waited, only this time they were waiting for one of them. Okay then, Mia thought, they just can wait for their answer. But apparently, Glen had another idea.

"Where is the jury of our peers?" he spoke up next to her. "What are we charged with? What right do you have to try us?

"We make the laws. We are the jury," the man in the mask said, in a deep, resonant bass voice. "We are the judge. You shall live and die by the power of this Court. Who is Melvin Foles?"

A deep calm came over Mia, she knew they were facing evil, and she knew between them they could counter it.

"I am Melvin Foles." Mia rose to her feet. She stood for a heartbeat, then two.

"I am Melvin Foles." Glen stood.

Mia let out her breath.

"I am Melvin Foles," Melvin said, also rising to his feet.

"I am Melvin Foles." Christian had some trouble rising as he couldn't put his full weight on his injured leg. Mia reached over, took his hand and helped him to his feet.

"I am Melvin Foles." Sally was the last, and her voice rang out and filled the room.

The woman on the dais frowned. The young black man furrowed his brow. The eyes behind the mask stared at each of them in turn.

"This is your response?" the woman asked. "You all are Melvin Foles?"

"Yes," they responded as one, which Mia took as a point in their favor. They were doing well, considering they hadn't had time to plan, and wouldn't have known what to prepare for. As long as they were protecting each other, they would be in accord.

"You all are willing to take responsibility for the crimes of Melvin Foles?"

"What crimes are those?" Mia's voice rang clear. "The crime of feeding the hungry? The crime of healing the sick? Which crime is it that we are to be punished for?"

"You are to be punished for the crime of wasting resources," the bass voice beyond the mask answered. "You defied us and healed a man we judged unworthy. The power of the Koupe Tribinal is absolute. Defiance always will be punished. You will be punished."

"And yet, you would commit that same crime," Sally called out. "We are a resource, one this city desperately needs, and yet you would punish us for doing good works in this godforsaken city. Will you then punish yourselves for punishing us? Or do you prefer to be known as hypocrites?"

Somewhere behind Mia, someone hissed. That had got a reaction. Well, good. Let's get more reaction.

"False justice is meted out by the cowards of this world," she said. "Only bullies drag people in off the street, try, convict, and punish them all in a moment. There are no judges here. You already have made up your minds. There is no trial, only a reckoning of your own making. You believe yourselves to be above your own laws. You rule as cruel dictators, too frightened to allow democracy to flourish."

"We are not above the law, we are the law," the masked man bellowed. "For who is there to keep the streets of this city safe if not for us?"

"But you don't keep the city safe," Melvin spoke up, although his voice was a little reedy with fear, Glen thought. "We've been set upon by thugs and criminals, and it was only a sort of neighborhood watch that rescued us. It is the citizens of this city that take care of each other, not you in your dank basement, doing your best to scare people into submission."

"What right have you to speak to us of leadership?" the man in the mask thundered. "You who hide in the night, healing the scum, dragging their bodies into the streets, stealing supplies needed for the people and keeping them for yourselves?"

"For the rich, you mean." Mia could hear the outrage in her own voice. "For those who can pay or give you favors. Not for the people, or by the people, but for your own gain, and those of your kind. Meanwhile, the rest of us are fighting entropy the best we can, without the help of those with power. Just like the meanest societies in all of history."

The woman looked as if she had been slapped. Shocked, outraged, and angry. *Surely I am not the first to speak back to her*, Mia thought. *Are the people of this city so cowed that they dare not speak up for themselves?*

The younger man on the far right looked thoughtful, not hurt or angered by her words. Pensive. If there came time for an appeal, he would be the one she would target. His eyes were intelligent and troubled. There was something about this process that didn't sit right with his worldview, she could tell, and that was a weakness she'd exploit.

At a signal from the woman, the men also rose. As they moved to exit the room, the woman admonished the guards not to let the prisoners leave.

And again they were waiting.

Find out what happens in part four! Available Now!

www.ingramcontent.com/pod-product-compliance
Lightning Source LLC
Chambersburg PA
CBHW032346090625
27971CB00007B/159